Table of Contents

The Crosspicking Guitar Technique Book

Introduction

Crosspicking guitar has immense roots. A culmination of many styles, artists, and instruments inspires the technique of crosspicking. Because the guitar itself dates back many centuries, as a member of the lute family, approaches to playing the guitar have been myriad and varied. Usually the style of music would dictate the approach. As to crosspicking, many styles of music can be effectively played so that crosspicking itself dictates the style. An example of this is to take a simple classical melody like "Greensleeves" and adapt it to a banjoistic roll (crosspicking) on the guitar; suddenly, the piece takes on a Bluegrass feel and becomes difficult to categorize.

With applied crosspicking technique, the guitar becomes a forceful solo instrument capable of filling a room with colorfully supported melodies. Crosspicking bombards the listener with a barrage of notes. As is similar to Bluegrass banjo, crosspicking guitar doesn't seem to pause for a breather. A continuous succession of notes pours forth establishing the melody while filling in all of the spaces with harmony notes. Not only does the guitar support itself, with spaces filled harmonically, but crosspicking technique works effectively for supporting other lead instruments and vocals. As an accomplished guitar player, you are or would be capable of varying the backup of an ensemble (band) with many colorful approaches; for example, one verse you may want to add bass-strum backup while the second verse you could apply a crosspicking backup.

The guitar, as one of the most versatile instruments in existence, has immersed triumphantly in many genres including: classical, rock, country, bluegrass, jazz, and new age music. No matter what style of music you enjoy playing, learning the many applicable possibilities of crosspicking will enhance your musical creativity. There are no limitations on how or where crosspicking can be applied. It's truly one approach to the guitar that can be adapted to any style of music.

This is a methodology book, which includes a songbook section, designed for the intermediate to advanced guitarist. It will offer you, as a guitar player, a new voice. Or, if you're already crosspicking, many new ideas can be added to your arsenal. Within the methodology chapters, each song includes a preparatory study that allows you the opportunity to gain a solid footing before attempting the piece itself. These studies can be applied in other areas as backup ideas, song ideas or takeoffs for improvisation. So, don't think of them only as exercises. Be creative and experimental. Upon completing the methodology section, this book also includes a full songbook section giving you an even wider repertoire to pursue.

This book was musically written in tablature (a number system)—you will not have to know, or learn, how to read music. If you know how to count, you can read tablature—just start from the beginning and pay careful attention to instructions and what each tab symbol indicates. All of the songs start with simple preparatory exercises that summarize any difficult passages; by accomplishing these exercises thoroughly, the songs will easily follow. Don't get impatient with your progress; remind yourself that you're playing the guitar because it's fun!

Mel Bay's
GUITAR CROSSPICKING TECHNIQUE

by Mickey Cochran

2 3 4 5 6 7 8 9 0

Visit us on the Web at www.melbay.com — E-mail us at email@melbay.com

Table of Contents

Part I: Guitar & Crosspicking Basics

Getting Oriented

How do you focus on a new technique and bypass the normal frustration involved with learning new habits and maybe even shedding old ones to accomplish the task? There are many approaches to playing the guitar; many of them haven't even been invented yet! The more you can learn about your chosen instrument, the closer you come to actualizing your musical goals. Whether you play the guitar as an accompanist or instrumentalist, your arsenal of licks, chords and techniques is what you depend on. If you haven't already, once you've incorporated crosspicking into your arsenal, you'll wonder how you've played so long without this colorful texture.

To become oriented in the task of learning crosspicking involves setting short-time goals. Become familiar with the foundation and build your skills with each exercise in the order they are taught. Reward yourself with the sense of accomplishment that follows after mastering a crosspicking exercise or arrangement. And, don't let anybody tell you that crosspicking is easy. There are times when you will hit the wall and feel like you're not getting anywhere fast. Your best strategy in this case is to go back over what you've learned up to this point and keep on practicing. Before long, you'll find yourself smoothly moving forward to other goals.

Enjoy The Journey

Practice Makes Perfect

Well we've all heard that maxim one too many times! Even so, this truism lives on. You cannot move from "a to b" without practicing. No one starts from the top of the mountain; some of us just climb faster than others.

Step 1: Set up a practice schedule.

The consequence: you'll see very little progress in accomplishing your goals. Keep a journal of what, when, and how much you practiced. Set up small goals to accomplish and notate your progress as you go along.

Step 2: Carry a road map.

If you want to reach the summit quickly, carry a road map. You need a guide to assist you in developing habits or technique to make accomplishing the task easier and more efficient. This book is one of many. Research your interests and start a library of instructional material that you can glean new songs and technique from.

Step 3: Make sure your tools are sufficient.

Your guitar does not necessarily have to be an expensive instrument to learn on. Although, if it's not set up properly, you'll become frustrated trying to accomplish any musical goals with it. For instance, if the instrument has a high action (strings being abnormally high off the fretboard), you will not be able to comfortably fret the notes making it impossible to crosspick with ease. If the saddle is not properly located, or the neck is out of alignment, your intonation (tuning) will be off making it difficult to tune your guitar. If you haven't up to now, I'd highly recommend taking your guitar to a luthier (instrument specialist) for proper setup.

Tuning, Strings & Things

Tuning Preparation

Ease of tuning your guitar is determined by many factors:

1. Intonation: If your saddle is not properly located, or your neck is warped, your guitar will become next to impossible to tune. To test whether your bridge is properly placed, or if your neck needs adjusting, try playing 12th fret harmonics on each string followed by fretting at the 12th fret. If the pitch does not match on any of the strings, then the saddle is not properly placed for intonation (which can be caused by a warped neck). One string may be closer than others indicating that the saddle is very close to where it should be but the individual strings aren't properly compensated. In either case, I recommend that you take your guitar to a luthier for proper setup.

2. Strings: If your strings are old, replace them. Strings become corroded and nicked over time making them very difficult to tune properly. If your strings are not properly weaved through the eye of your tuning keys, you may have slippage causing the instrument to be constantly going out of tune. Consult with a luthier or music store on how to properly replace your strings.

3. Frets: Worn frets can cause many intonation problems. Usually fret wear occurs at the first five frets of your instrument. Look closely for grooves directly under where your strings are fretted to determine if you may have this problem. If so, have a luthier replace or file them as may be required.

4. Keys: Tuning keys do wear out! The gears can be damaged causing the revolutions to vary.

5. Nut: Many times a string can get caught in the process of tuning it within the groove of the nut. To remedy this, try placing a small amount of graphite within the groove. If this doesn't correct the problem, you'll have to take it in to a luthier for replacement or repair.

String Gauges

The string gauge will influence playability of your guitar greatly. Crosspicking is such a demanding technique for stretches and chording that it is critical to use either light or medium gauge strings. Heavy gauge strings would not be recommended for crosspicking due to their weightiness. I use medium gauge since there's a sacrifice in volume when using light gauge. Although, if you're just starting out, or have never attempted crosspicking before, I recommend light gauge strings. If you want, upon accomplishing the technique of crosspicking, you can graduate to medium gauge strings. Light gauge strings are definitely easier to fret, you'll find yourself not fighting with the instrument as much as you would with medium gauge strings.

Strings also come in many alloys. Crosspicking sounds great on bright, brassy strings. Try a phosphor bronze alloy if you like this characteristic. Otherwise, if you prefer a more mellow tone, try nickel wound strings. As there are so many stylists, there are also many different tastes in strings. The choice usually reflects the artist's taste and will usually become a signature of that particular artist. Experiment and discover what works best for you.

To keep your strings sounding bright and easy to tune, clean them often. Consult with your local music store for what products work best for this purpose.

How to Play Harmonics

Natural harmonics occur at the 5th, 7th, and 12th frets of your guitar. This division also repeats past the 12th fret. By placing your finger lightly above any string above these particular frets while striking the string with your pick, you'll hear a bell-like tone ring out. If not, keep experimenting by touching the string simultaneously as you pick it. Notice that by lifting the finger slightly, directly after picking the note, you will create a louder bell tone.

Tuning Methodology

Methods of Tuning

The guitar is tuned in fourths overall (except for the "G" to "B" strings). From the 6th string (E Lowest), each string is tuned a fourth above the previous (except for the "G" to "B" strings which are tuned a third apart).

There are many approaches that can be utilized effectively for tuning your guitar. The important thing is to know at least two approaches so that you can verify that it's tuned properly with a second approach. Before we learn these approaches, you'll need a starting reference for one of the strings. The best tool to have at your disposal is a tuning fork that vibrates at 440 Cycles equaling "A". This is the same pitch as the 5th string "A" except one octave higher. After matching up the tuning fork with your "A" string, you're prepared to utilize the following tuning methods. (Another great investment would be an electronic guitar tuner.)

Tuning Method 1 by Fretting

Step 1: Place your first finger (index finger) on the 5th fret of the "A" string (5th string)—This note is "D" and should match your 4th string "D". Tune the "D" string until the pitch matches the "A" string, fretted at the 5th fret.

Step 2: Now, place your first finger on the 5th fret of the "D" string (4th string)—This note is "G" and should match your 3rd string. Tune the "G" string until it matches your "D" string fretted at the 5th fret.

Step 3: Place your first finger on the 4th fret of the "G" string (3rd string)—This note is "B" and should match your 2nd string "B". Tune the "B" string until it matches your "G" string fretted at the 4th fret.

Step 4: Place your first finger on the 5th fret of the "B" string (2nd string)—This note is "E" and should match your 1st string "E". Tune the "E" string until it matches your "B" string fretted at the 5th fret.

Step 5: Now, the only string left to tune would be the low "E" 6th. Since our "A" 5th string was already tuned to the tuning fork, you can match the "E" fretted at the 5th fret to the "A" string.

Upon completing this first tuning method, you're now ready to verify if it's correct by utilizing a second tuning method.

Tuning Method 2 by Harmonics

This method requires the ability to play "harmonics". Instructions for learning to play harmonics are in the side-bar of the previous page.

Step 1: Play a harmonic above the 12th fret of the "E" string. This pitch should match the 5th string fretted at the 7th fret. If it doesn't, attempt to fine tune the 5th string before moving on to Step 2.

Step 2: Play a harmonic above the 12th fret of the "A" string. This pitch should match the 4th string fretted at the 7th fret. If it doesn't, attempt to fine tune the 4th string before moving on to Step 3.

Step 3: Play a harmonic above the 12th fret of the "D" string. This pitch should match the 3rd string fretted at the 7th fret. If it doesn't, attempt to fine tune the 3rd string before moving on to Step 4.

Step 4: Play a harmonic above the 12th fret of the "G" string. This pitch should match the 2nd string fretted at the 8th fret. If it doesn't, attempt to fine tune the 2nd string before moving on. For the E string, repeat the same pattern illustrated in Step 1-3

Now that you've verified how close you came with the Tuning Method 1, try going back to it to see if it is tuned consistently. If not, your intonation may be considerably off, or you still may need practice at tuning. Developing an ear to determine pitch can be accomplished by listening carefully and always referencing where you're at by fretting notes above and below the note being tuned. Experiment and take your time. (If you're a beginner at tuning, your best investment would be an electronic guitar tuner.)

Guitar Tablature Staff & Numbers

Tablature is one of the oldest forms of notating music. It's a number system that follows a simple logic for guitar: each number represents the fret distance and each line represents a guitar string. Of course, other considerations include timing and embellishments. Please pay careful attention to the following tablature indications and refer back to them whenever necessary.

The Staff

The staff consists of 6 lines each representing a string on the guitar. The top line represents the low "E" string; the bottom line represents the high "E" string.

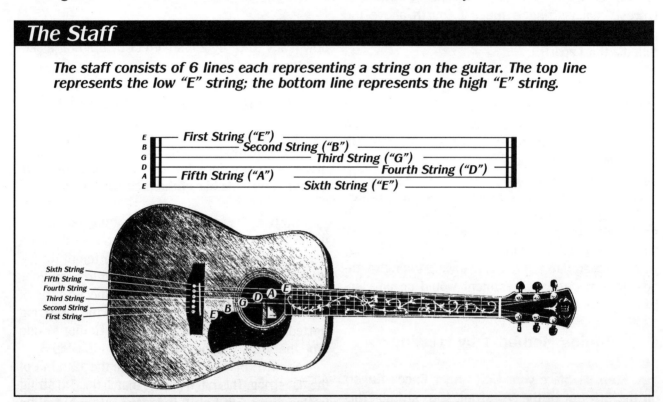

The Numbers

Every note is indicated by a number representing the distance of the fret from the nut. For instance: A "0" indicates that the string is to be played open, while a "3" indicates that the finger is to be placed behind the 3rd fret before picking the string.

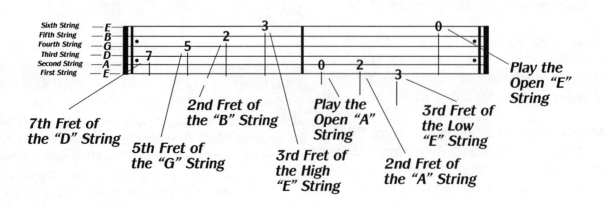

Guitar Fretboard

The guitar fretboard corresponds very easily to tablature staff. An example of the first 5 frets are illustrated below with the corresponding number indications for tablature.

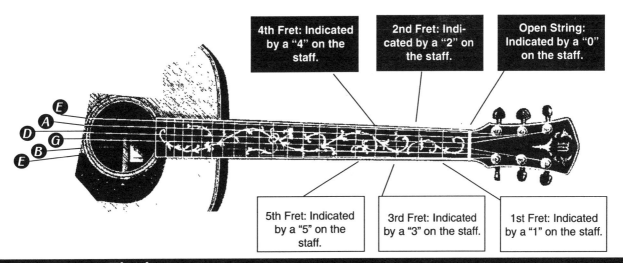

4th Fret: Indicated by a "4" on the staff.

2nd Fret: Indicated by a "2" on the staff.

Open String: Indicated by a "0" on the staff.

5th Fret: Indicated by a "5" on the staff.

3rd Fret: Indicated by a "3" on the staff.

1st Fret: Indicated by a "1" on the staff.

Tablature Timing

All forms of music notation has a system of symbols that translates the rhythm and timing of a song. Tablature borrows these symbols from standard notation so that it becomes a complete music language and can stand on its own without the player having to hear a recording of the piece before attempting to play it. Most all of the tunes in this book follow the standard 4 beats per measure with each beat represented by a quarter note. This is indicated at the beginning of each piece by a ¾ symbol. The top number represents how many beats per measure, and the bottom number represents the type of note that receives the beat. For our uses, you will only be required to tap your foot four times for each measure.

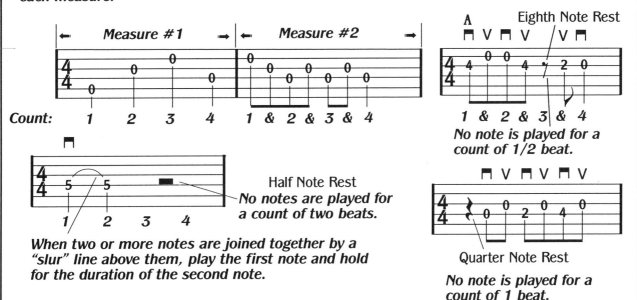

When two or more notes are joined together by a "slur" line above them, play the first note and hold for the duration of the second note.

Half Note Rest
No notes are played for a count of two beats.

No note is played for a count of 1/2 beat.

Quarter Note Rest

No note is played for a count of 1 beat.

Timing (cont.)

One way to ensure that you're playing in correct timing is by keeping your eye on the Down & Up Stroke symbols. If a note is joined to another with a slur note, you'll only see one stroke symbol for the first note; the duration of the following note is only held for the sustain of the first note. Anytime you see a rest symbol following a note directly, the note should be deadened for the duration of the rest symbol. To do this, simply lift your fretting finger up slightly directly after picking the note, or if it's an open string, mute it with your right hand.

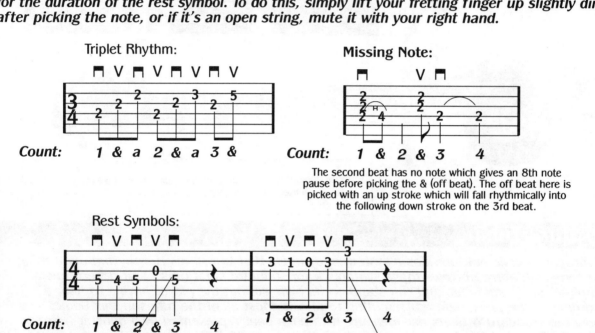

Triplet Rhythm:

Count: 1 & a 2 & a 3 &

Missing Note:

Count: 1 & 2 & 3 4

The second beat has no note which gives an 8th note pause before picking the & (off beat). The off beat here is picked with an up stroke which will fall rhythmically into the following down stroke on the 3rd beat.

Rest Symbols:

Count: 1 & 2 & 3 4   1 & 2 & 3 4

These notes are only held for one beat and followed with lifting the finger so that the note does not ring out for the fourth beat.

Timing is very relative to the feel of a musical piece. This brings us to a very important point, the soul or feel of a musical piece cannot be captured by symbols on a page. It is up to the musician to infuse the song with his own interpretation of what mood he or she is trying to communicate. The mood and feel of a guitar piece is influenced by many factors including: timing, speed, which note is accented, medium (what type of pick is being used), gauge of strings, etc. Before attempting to read a piece, it is recommended to listen to the musical piece, or be already familiar with the melody, so that you at least have a good idea of what it sounds like. From there, you'll have artistic license for interpreting the piece.

Timing is of the Essence

Guitar Tablature Pick Strokes

Pick Strokes

There are only two pick strokes that can be accomplished with a flatpick: the "up stroke" and the "down stroke". In most flatpicking instances the down stroke would be played on the down beat and the up stroke would be played on the off beat. This is fairly consistent with crosspicking, although there are also many instances where the down beat would be played by an up stroke depending on the pattern involved. Below is an example of the standard approach including pick stroke symbols.

⊓ = Down Stroke

V = Up Stroke

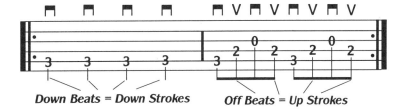

Down Beats = Down Strokes   Off Beats = Up Strokes

NOTE: Because crosspicking is very dependent on what direction is the pick stroke, all pieces and exercises include the pick stroke symbols for up and down. The rhythm and feel of the piece is established by the pick direction. Notes that fall naturally under an accent are accommodated by the pick stroke which greatly influences which notes are emphasized. The pick strokes notated are not necessarily the only direction to use; for instance, instead of down/up/down/up, try down/up/up for a different feel. The main goal with your picking hand would be to gain total independence.

The Metronome

The metronome is a very useful tool for determining the tempo of a tune. Of course the alternative is to listen to the piece being performed and match the tempo from the recording. The metronome is still a great tool for other purposes such as learning to keep good time. Each arrangement in this book has a box with the target tempo indicated by a quarter note followed by an "=" and a number. The number is the setting for the metronome. Target tempo is what you will be striving for as you practice. Normally you'll have to start out playing the arrangement slowly and gain speed as you become comfortable with the arrangement.

The ultimate speed of the piece is indicated by the metronome setting. Start slowly and work up to the metronome setting.

Target Tempo:
♩ = 200

This metronome setting is for 200. Each quarter note (♩) represents one beat. The number will always equal how many beats occur within one minute.

Tablature Symbols

It is not necessary to attempt to memorize all of the symbols at this point. Just glance over them now and when encountering them in the arrangements refer back to this section for clarification.

Chord Indications

Chord indications are placed above the arrangement and establish the progression of the piece. It helps to become familiar with the chord progression before attempting to learn the arrangement.

Chord Symbols are Placed Directly Above the Measure

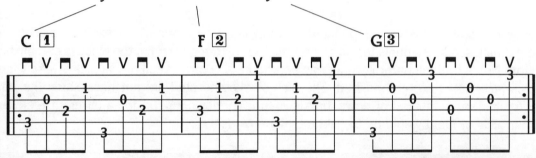

The below excerpt shows an Em ending chord that is strummed with a down stroke. It is strummed only once and held for two beats.

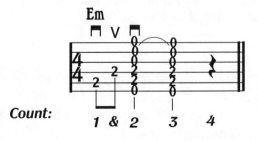

Guitar Tablature Endings

Endings

Many tunes have "First Endings" and "Second Endings" that are indicated by the numbers "1" and "2". To properly play through these endings, simply return to the double dot upon playing the "First Ending"; while playing through it a second time, skip the "First Ending" playing only the "Second Ending" and, unless otherwise indicated, continue on through the piece .

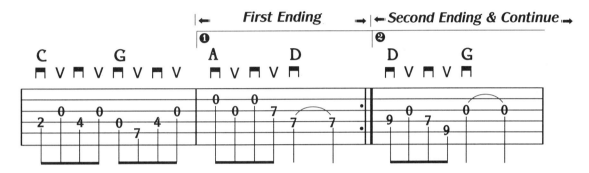

Song Endings are indicated by double lines without dots. At this point, you may optionally start the piece over or call it a take.

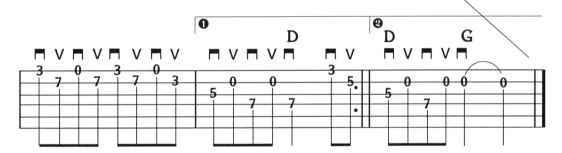

Section Endings are indicated by two dots—at this point, go back to the beginning of the section where the two dots start and repeat the entire section one time. Continue past the two dots after repeating the section.

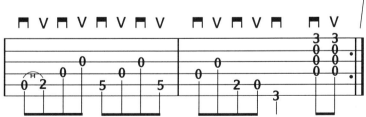

Attack Symbols

The following indications are for the many ways that a string can be attacked (played) by the flatpick. These embellishments add color, texture and variety to the musical piece.

HAMMER-ONS

Hammer-ons are indicated by an "H" and a slur line. A hammer-on will always be going up in pitch not down.

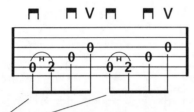

The first note, on the open "A" string, is picked with a down stroke while the second note is created with a forceful hammer with the fretting second finger.

PULL-OFFS

Pull-offs are indicated by a "P" and a slur line. Pull-offs are essentially the reverse of hammer-ons. Your fretting hand will pull off of the designated note and string, thereby creating the following note/s without picking the string but once.

The first note is picked with a down stroke while the second note is created with a pull-off motion of the fretting finger.

HARMONICS

Harmonics are created by lightly touching the string with your left finger while at the same time picking the string with your right hand. Natural harmonics can only be created at designated fret positions that divide the distance from the nut to the bridge.

Harmonics are indicated by a down stroke symbol with a dot in the center.

SLIDES

Slides are indicated by an "S" with a diagonal line between two notes. Simply slide your fretting finger up to the next note indicated after picking the first note.

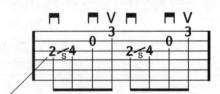

Slides are indicated by a slash with an "S" underneath. In this example, pick the first note as a down stroke and then slide up to the 4th fret on the off beat.

Chord Diagrams

Chords

Chord inversions (positions) are laid out in both tablature and chord diagrams. Whenever you see more than one number aligned in tablature, you will be playing a chord (notes simultaneously played or fretted). Be careful to pay attention to the down or up stroke indicated when playing chords.

TABLATURE CHORD INDICATIONS

When you see any numbers placed on top of one another, a chord position is being illustrated.

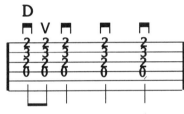

Count: 1   &   2   3   4

All down stroke symbols designate that the chord is to be strummed in a downward motion, the up stoke symbol requires that the chord be strummed in an upward motion.

CHORD DIAGRAMS

Chord diagrams are on every preparatory study page. By careful study and use of the hand positions illustrated, the arrangements are less difficult to deal with.

❶ =First Finger
❷ =Second Finger
❸ =Third Finger
❹ =Fourth Finger

1st →

A number with an arrow indicates what fret position that the chord starts at.

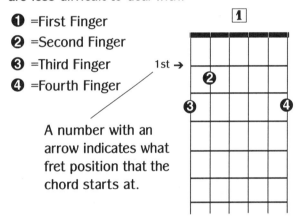

Each exercise page displays chord positions that are utilized throughout the studies and songs. Open strings utilized (not fretted by the left hand) will be indicated on the tablature by "O's".

1st →

Fret Position

Strings

Number Relates to Positions Also Indicated In Exercises

5th →

5th Fret Past First Position

Number Relates to Positions Also Indicated In Exercises

1st →

Finger Positions

Horizontal Lines Represent Frets

Nut
First
Position

❶=First Finger   ❷=Second Finger   ❸ =Third Finger   ❹ =Fourth Finger

Useful Tools

More On The Metronome

Invented by J. N. Mälzel in 1816, the metronome is invaluable during the learning process. Not only does it measure the exact tempo of the arrangements enclosed (settings are indicated at the top of each piece), but it becomes an indispensable tool for measuring your progress with the exercises and studies. By starting out on low settings, you'll be able to learn the exercise with an even tempo establishing a good foundation for playing the exercises up-tempo.

The metronome will also give you an inner sense of good timing that will reflect whenever you get together with other musicians. Keep a metronome by your side whenever you're practicing!

Picks

Picks come in many sizes, thicknesses and shapes. Crosspicking demands a lot of a pick. Try to avoid picks that are too thin (light) for they have no projection and slap with a clicking sound on the strings. Use a medium to heavy pick for better volume and more control. As far as size is concerned, it should come down to personal preference. Even though, avoid using tiny picks; they don't have much area to grab a string which can cause a loss in dynamic control. Smaller picks are less likely to attack a string with force on a guitar. You need to be able to get behind the strings with a medium to large-size pick in order to pluck the string for increased volume.

Types of Metronomes

Traditional Pendulum Version	**Modern-Day Electronic Version**
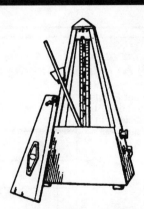	
This version operates by a windup pendulum along with a weight that adjusts the speed.	This digital version operates by touchpad controls and consists of an LCD Display that indicates the tempo along with an audio output emitting a beep for every beat.

This is only a sampling of the many varieties of metronomes available today.

Right Hand Technique

Right-Hand Position

There are as many ways for positioning the right hand as there are guitar players. Many of the positions limit the right hand from moving freely. This restricts the playing capability of the right hand and will limit speed and dexterity. With crosspicking, it is critical that the right hand is loosely positioned above the strings so that it can move completely free of any obstruction. For instance, many guitar players rest the heel of the hand on the bridge; this restricts the right-hand picking movement and does not allow the hand to take advantage of playing closer to the fingerboard for a mellower tone.

Crosspicking technique can be accomplished efficiently by keeping the wrist loose. Imagine trying to jump from string to string for every other note with a stiff wrist. Although, it can be done, your whole forearm has to move for every note; whereas, with a loose wrist, the movement is much more concentrated and can be easily accomplished with minimal movement. The forearm does not need to be completely stationary, in fact, by playing with both a loose wrist and forearm, you'll have optimal movement for speed and efficiency.

How to Properly Hold Your Pick

There are many ways that the pick is welded. Some contribute to effective technique while many others will impede technique. After getting comfortable with playing with a loose wrist, how you hold your pick should fall into place. No two players have the exact same muscle and build for hands and arms. Therefore, what works for one individual may not work for another. There still are common principles that apply to everyone.

1. You should never have to grab your pick tightly. This will only tighten up your muscles unnecessarily and will reflect in your playing with tension and tightness.

2. You should never choke your pick to the point that there's a limited surface for it to strike the string. This will minimize the ability to utilize dynamics (volume control), will limit accuracy, and will make it difficult to strike the string with force for added volume.

3. The pick angle should always be flat in relation to the strings. If not, you'll gain transients (pick noise) as the pick rubs against wound strings. Sometimes, you'll want this effect to utilize as coloring, although, usually only on rare occasions.

Wrist Loosening Exercise

When throwing a Frisbee, or dealing out a deck of cards, the wrist is usually completely loose in the process. Now apply this same looseness to your guitar by playing a tremolo, rapid succession of up and down pick strokes, on each string. A tremolo is a rapid down-and-up movement of the pick against a string that will give the impression of a long continuous tone. Your forearm will move slightly in the process even with your wrist completely loose. Practice this technique until you feel confident that you're playing with a loose wrist. If you're tiring quickly, you're probably not using enough wrist movement and need to focus on being totally relaxed when approaching this exercise. You'll know you've accomplished the exercise properly when you do not tire easily and find yourself playing the tremolo without any concentrated effort.

Crosspicking Exercises

Introductory Arpeggios within Crosspicking

The following exercises will establish a solid foundation for the crosspicking arrangements to follow. It is critical to develop good right-hand technique in order to crosspick with total independence. Accomplish these exercises in the order that they are given before attempting any of the arrangements in this book.

The first exercise involves only the right hand; no left-hand fretting will be required. This exercise will allow you to focus on right-hand movement without the distraction of having to fret with the left hand. This exercise pattern is essentially arpeggios focusing on alternating the bass. Pay careful attention to the repeat symbols...each measure is a study in itself. Become completely comfortable with the first measure before moving on to the second measure.

Alternating Bass Roll

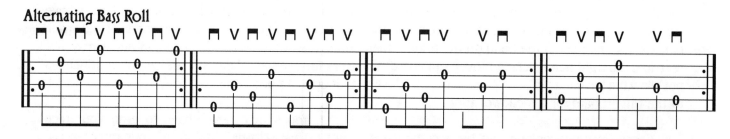

Before moving on to other studies, try playing these exercises with your eyes closed. You should be able to cross over from exercise to exercise without stopping or accidentally hitting the wrong string. Once you're comfortable with this pattern, and have it completely memorized, you may continue onward where we'll be attempting the same patterns with applied chord progressions.

Alternating Bass Pattern with Chord Progression

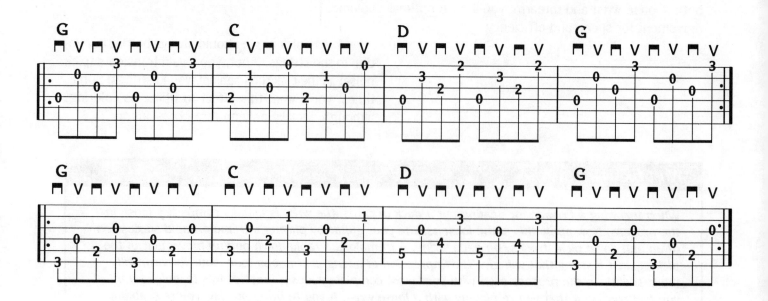

Crosspicking Exercises

Further Chord Progressions with Alternating Bass Patterns

The following exercises introduces a variety of chord progressions utilizing the alternating bass pattern. If you've memorized the preceding exercises, you now should only have to concentrate on fretting the positions with the left hand. Attempt to accomplish these chord progressions, with the alternating bass pattern, along with an even tempo; there should not be a pause during any chord change.

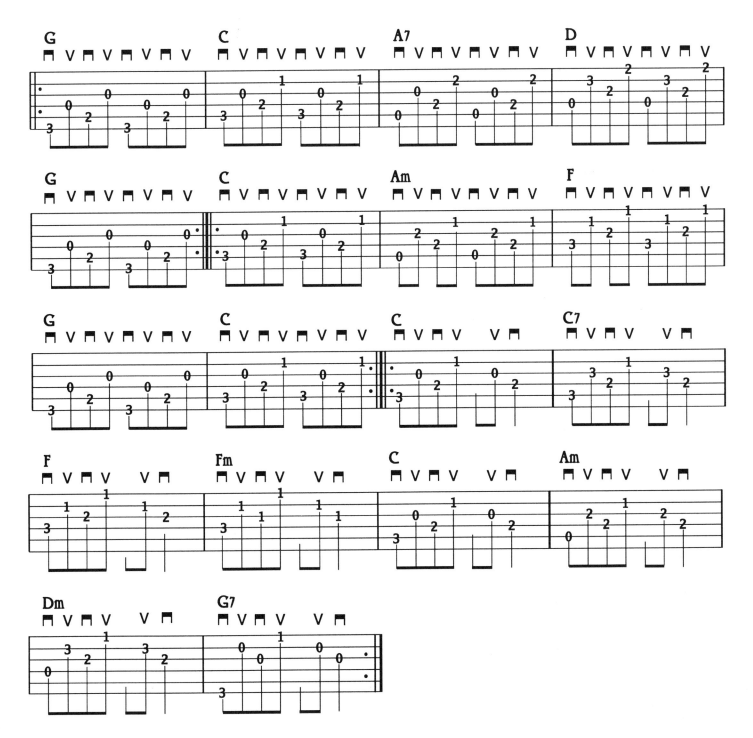

Crosspicking Exercises

Forward Rolls

We are now going to focus on the many other crosspicking patterns that will be utilized throughout the book. After learning these patterns thoroughly, we'll also be applying them to chord progressions so that you'll be developing your left and right hand coordination. The following forward rolls are commonly heard in banjo playing.

Forward Roll

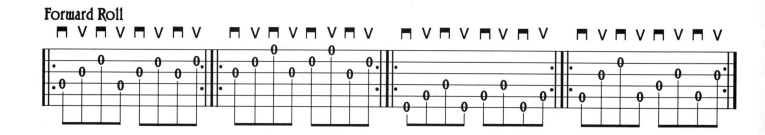

Forward Roll with Applied G Chord Progression

After you've mastered the above patterns...try applying the G chord progression as follows. Do not attempt the chord progression below without first having mastered the above forward roll exercises. To determine if you have mastered your right hand forward roll pattern, try playing the pattern without looking. Make sure you have an even tempo; there should be no pause between notes whatsoever.

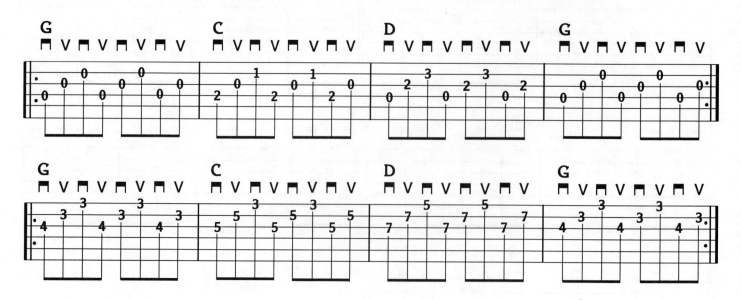

Forward Rolls (cont.)

All of these variations may be applied to any number of chord progressions you'd like to try. A surefire way to become comfortable with these rolls is to experiment with them within other chord progressions before moving on. Always consider the many possibilities that await you after memorizing these rolls. Try adding new life to old songs by applying them within familiar contexts.

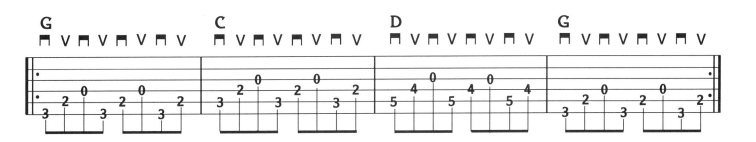

Crosspicking Exercises

Reverse Rolls

The reverse roll is essentially a backward forward roll. Again, these are commonly heard in banjo playing. Try playing these exercises with the down/up picking pattern shown and with a down/up/up picking pattern. Learn to gain complete independence in your right hand so that you're not locked into any one pattern.

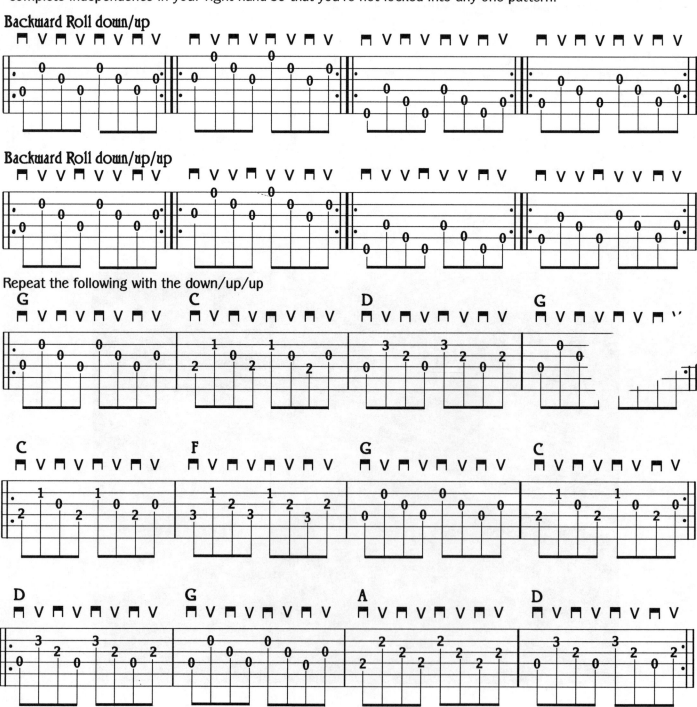

Reverse Rolls (cont.)

Reverse Roll with Applied Chord Progression
Repeat the following with the down/up/up

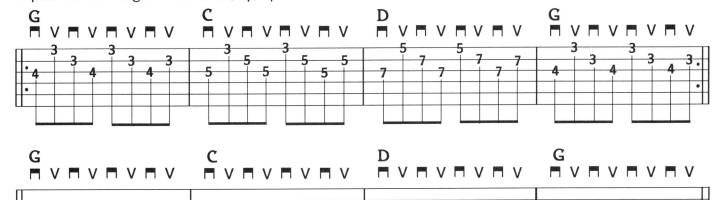

Jay Castleberry on a Tennessee Top-Tension

Crosspicking Exercises

Forward/Reverse Rolls

Here we're going to combine our previous two study patterns into one: the Forward/Reverse Roll. Another "banjoistic" pattern that will giving any piece of music a driving feel. Please note, we're also going to include our first melodic pattern that's a variation of the Forward/Reverse Roll. Notice the fourth measure below...this is a melodic pattern that's a sampling of what's to come in our song studies.

Forward/Reverse

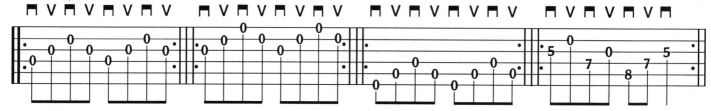

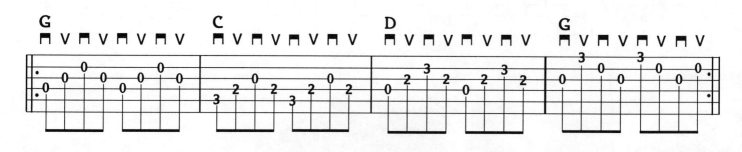

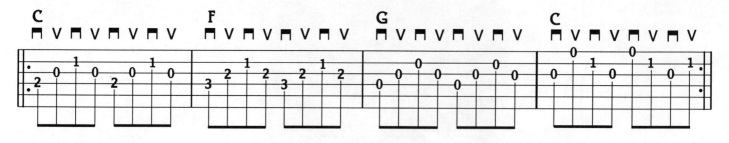

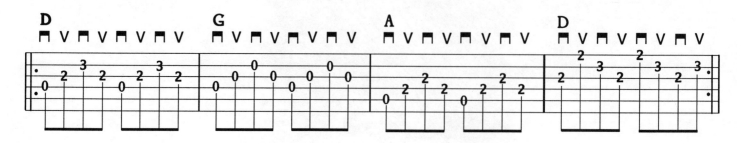

Crosspicking Exercises

The Capitan Gap New Mexico

Gibson Models: Buddy Holly J-45 and Everly Brothers

Crosspicking Bluegrass Style

Wildwood Flower

Home Sweet Home

Under the Double Eagle

John Hardy

Redwing

Grandfather's Clock

Wildwood Flower
Preparatory Study Notes

General Guidelines: Because of the many forward and reverse rolls utilized throughout, this arrangement has bluegrass banjo overtones. Keep the rhythm even and be careful not to rush the notes. The forward rolls can have a tendency to jump ahead of the tempo since they are easier to perform fast. If you're not practicing along with a metronome, try tapping your foot to ensure an even rhythm. Above all, accomplish all of the preparatory study notes before attempting the piece itself.

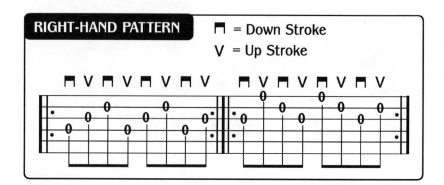

RIGHT-HAND PATTERN   ⊓ = Down Stroke   V = Up Stroke

RIGHT-HAND PATTERN WITH CHORD EXERCISE

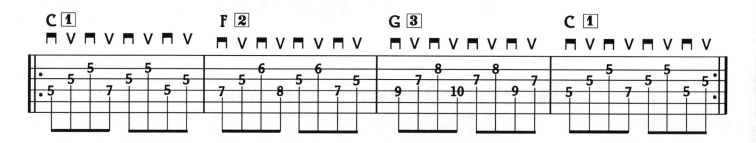

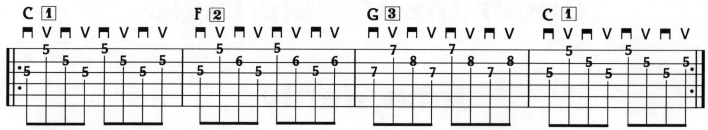

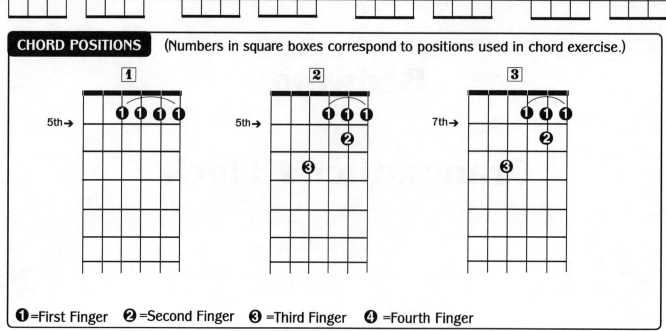

CHORD POSITIONS   (Numbers in square boxes correspond to positions used in chord exercise.)

❶=First Finger   ❷=Second Finger   ❸=Third Finger   ❹=Fourth Finger

Wildwood Flower
Preparatory Study Notes (cont.)

RIGHT-HAND PATTERN

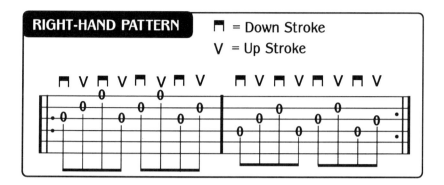

Of Noted Interest: The Carter Family had written many songs which today are considered standards. "Wildwood Flower" was quickly adapted as "the first tune to learn on acoustic guitar" by generations of folk guitarists. Mother Maybelle Carter does a beautiful autoharp rendition of this melody on the historic *Will The circle Be Unbroken* recording produced by William McEuen.

RIGHT-HAND PATTERN WITH CHORD EXERCISE

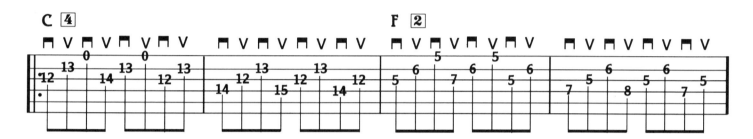

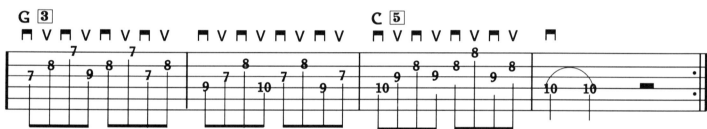

CHORD POSITIONS

(Numbers in square boxes correspond to positions used in chord exercise.)

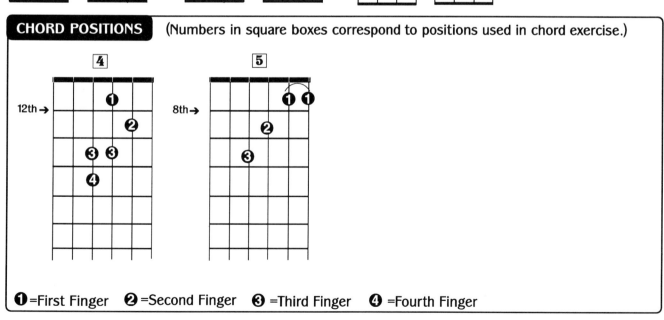

❶ =First Finger   ❷ =Second Finger   ❸ =Third Finger   ❹ =Fourth Finger

Wildwood Flower (Variation 1)

(A.P. CARTER)

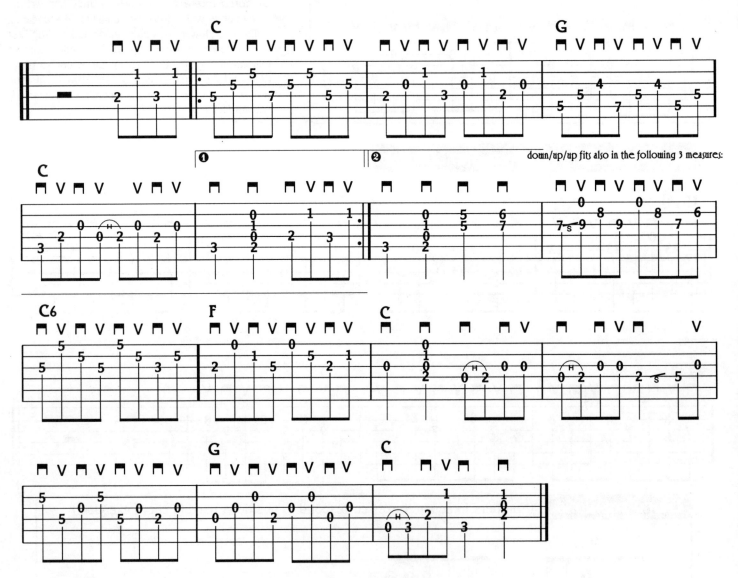

Wildwood Flower (Variation 2)

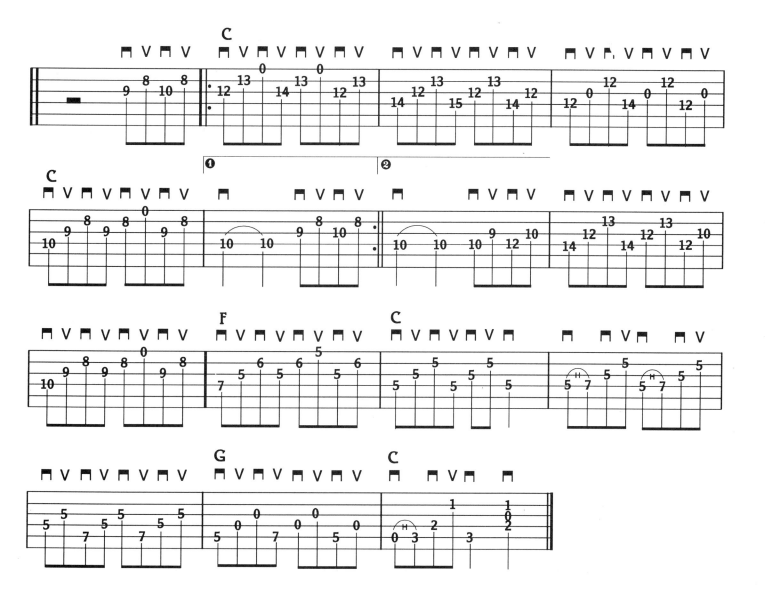

Bluegrass Style

Home Sweet Home
Preparatory Study Notes

General Guidelines: Before attempting the chord exercise, the right-hand pattern should be memorized and mastered. Keep the tempo even—there should be no pause whatsoever between any of the notes. Start off slowly, don't rush. Make sure you have all of the chord patterns memorized and can switch between them comfortably and efficiently. Notice how a few of the finger positions can remain stationary when switching from chord to chord. All that is required is to slide the fingers to the new position.

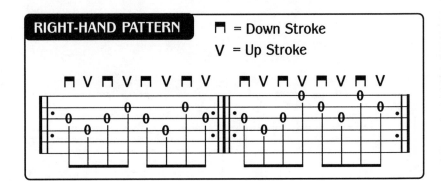

RIGHT-HAND PATTERN

⊓ = Down Stroke
V = Up Stroke

RIGHT-HAND PATTERN WITH CHORD EXERCISE

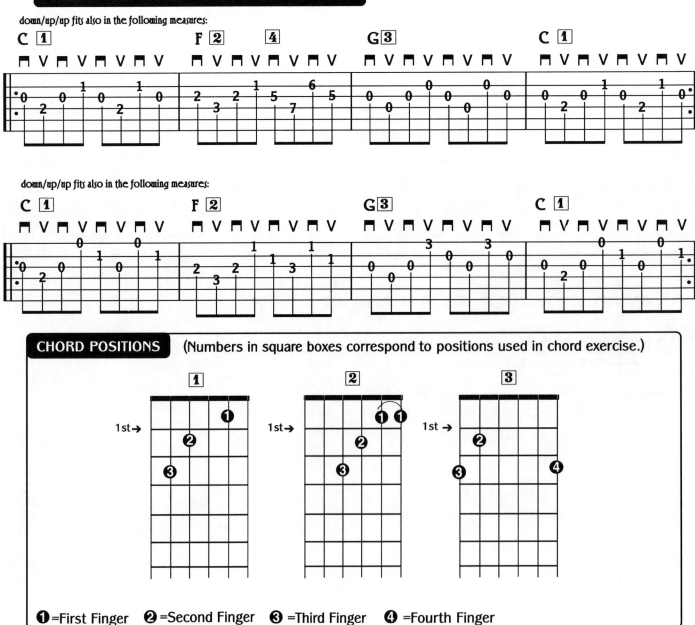

down/up/up fits also in the following measures:

C ①   F ②   ④   G ③   C ①

down/up/up fits also in the following measures:

C ①   F ②   G ③   C ①

CHORD POSITIONS (Numbers in square boxes correspond to positions used in chord exercise.)

①   ②   ③

❶ =First Finger   ❷ =Second Finger   ❸ =Third Finger   ❹ =Fourth Finger

Home Sweet Home
Preparatory Study Notes (cont.)

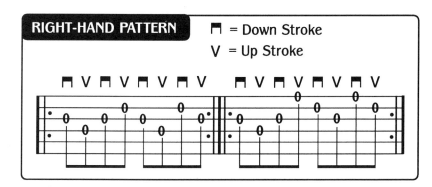

RIGHT-HAND PATTERN   ⊓ = Down Stroke
V = Up Stroke

Of Noted Interest: Dan Crary performs crosspicking guitar in a powerful way. His arrangement of "Home Sweet Home" in *Deacon Dan Crary's Flatpicking Guitar Technique* book is simple and effective. Glean new ideas by listening and studying at every opportunity to how a guitarist arranges and performs crosspicking.

Difficult Passages:

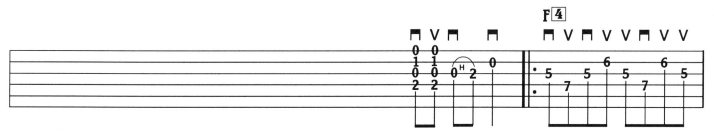

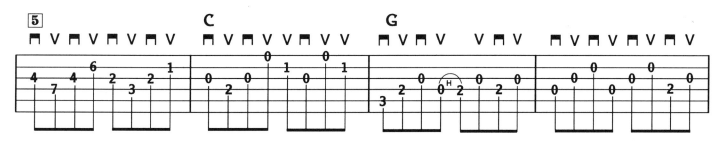

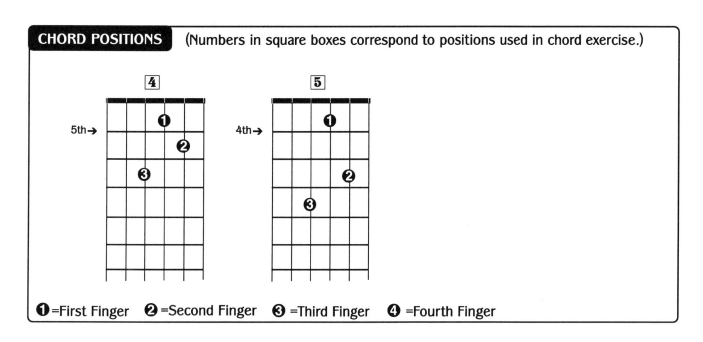

CHORD POSITIONS   (Numbers in square boxes correspond to positions used in chord exercise.)

❶=First Finger   ❷=Second Finger   ❸=Third Finger   ❹=Fourth Finger

Home Sweet Home

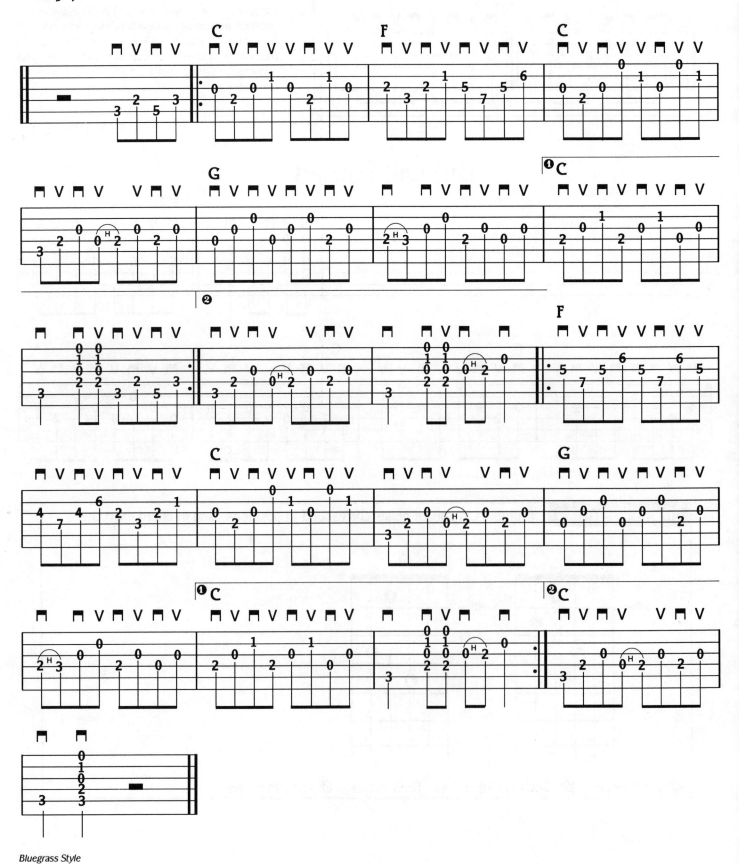

Bluegrass Style

'Mid pleasures and palaces though we may roam,
Be it ever so humble, there's no place like home.

Under The Double Eagle
Preparatory Study Notes

General Guidelines: Play this tune at a moderate pace with a "march" feel. Notice the "ragtime turnaround" in part II with the B6 chord! Try experimenting with other rolls over this same chord pattern.

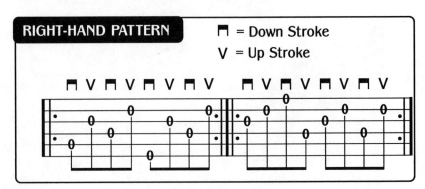

RIGHT-HAND PATTERN   ⊓ = Down Stroke
   V = Up Stroke

RIGHT-HAND PATTERN WITH CHORD EXERCISE

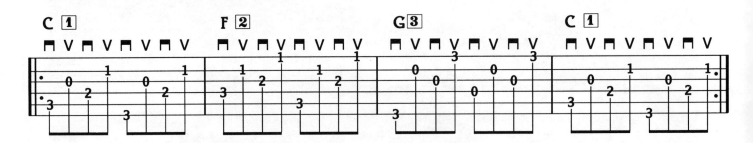

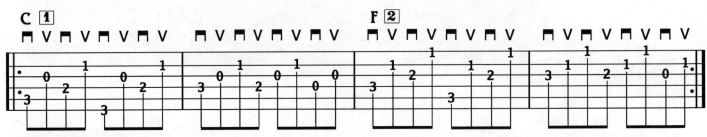

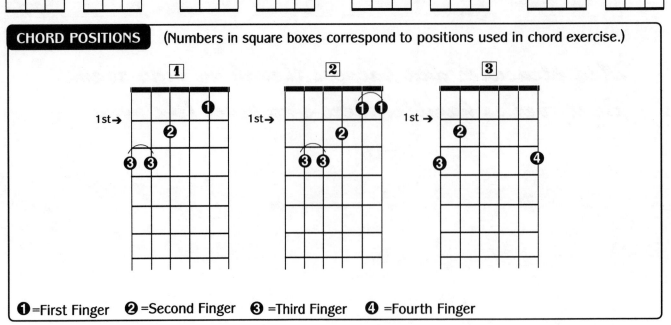

CHORD POSITIONS   (Numbers in square boxes correspond to positions used in chord exercise.)

❶=First Finger   ❷=Second Finger   ❸=Third Finger   ❹=Fourth Finger

Under The Double Eagle
Preparatory Study Notes (cont.)

RIGHT-HAND PATTERN

⊓ = Down Stroke
V = Up Stroke

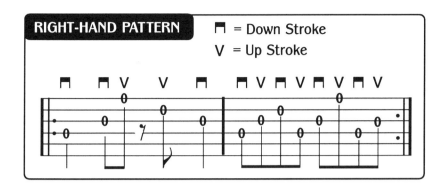

Of Noted Interest: Composed by Josef Franz Wagner in 1903 for marching band, this tune has been adapted by other genres and probably has had thousands of conceived arrangements. The original composition consisted of four parts. Today, the standard arrangement only consists of two parts.

RIGHT-HAND PATTERN WITH CHORD EXERCISE

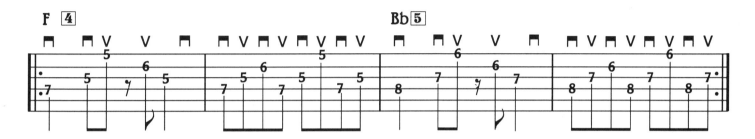

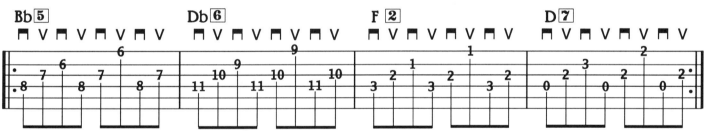

CHORD POSITIONS (Numbers in square boxes correspond to positions used in chord exercise.)

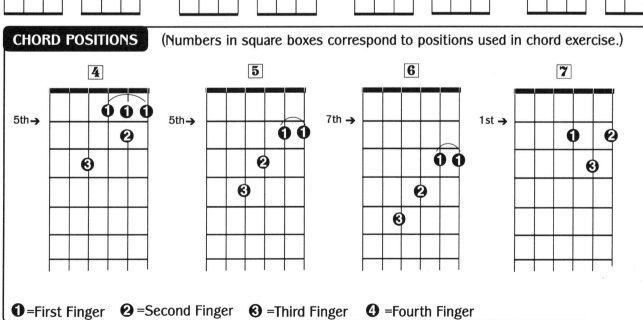

❶=First Finger   ❷=Second Finger   ❸=Third Finger   ❹=Fourth Finger

Under The Double Eagle

4/4 Target Tempo: ♩ = 200   A Part: Key of C   B Part: Key of F

(Josef Franz Wagner)

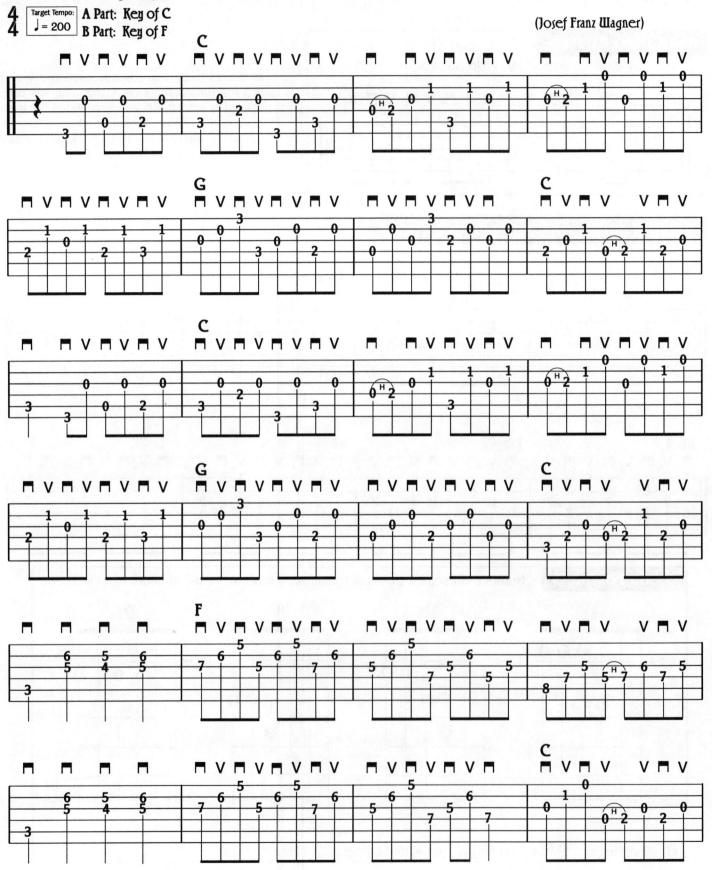

Under The Double Eagle (Continued)

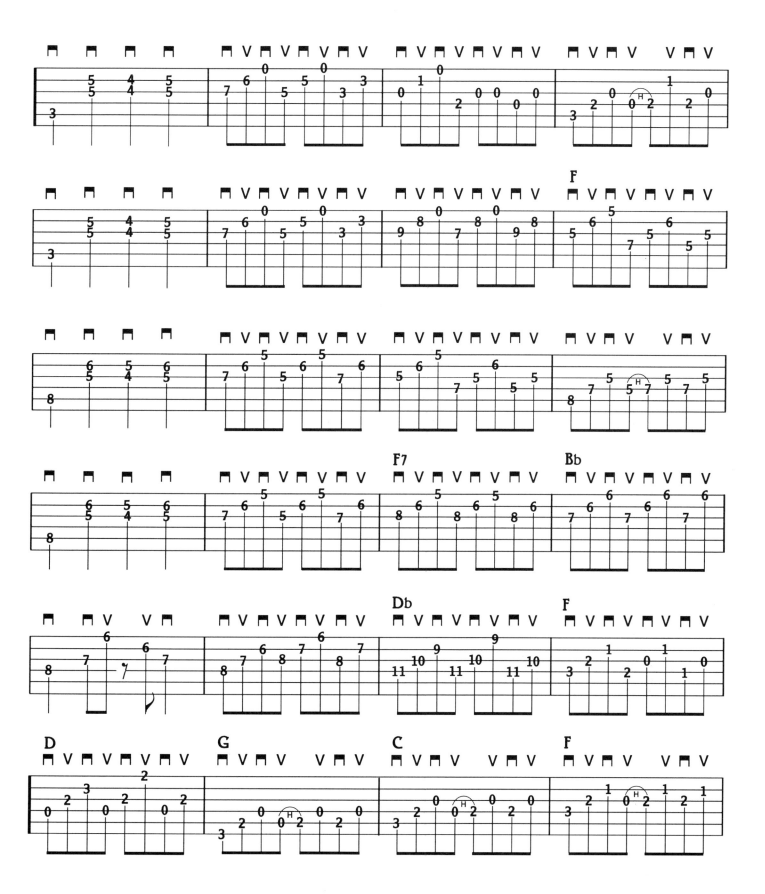

Bluegrass Style

Under The Double Eagle (Continued)

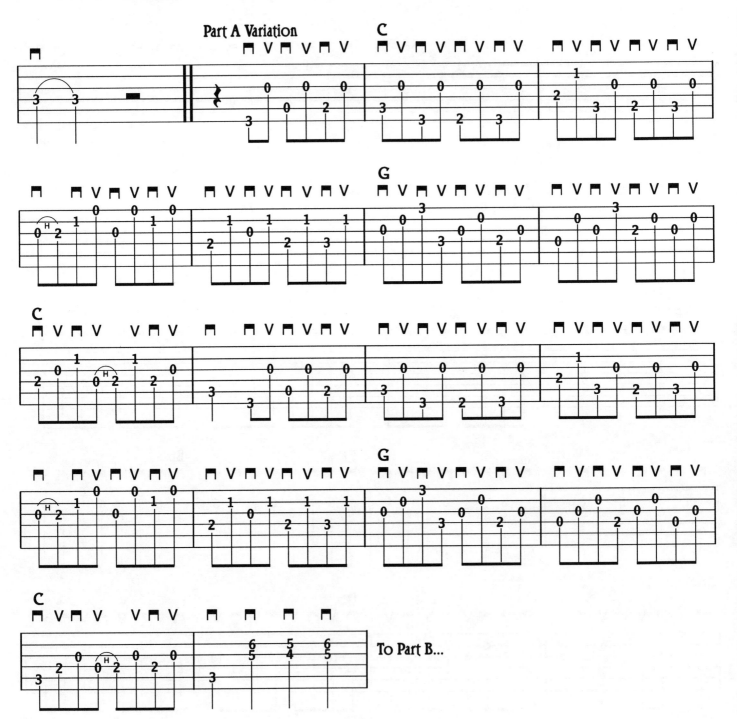

To Part B...

Bluegrass Style

John Hardy
Preparatory Study Notes

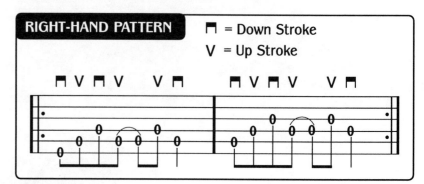

RIGHT-HAND PATTERN

☐ = Down Stroke

V = Up Stroke

General Guidelines: This arrangement is as banjoistic as you'll ever achieve with a guitar. Based mostly on forward rolls, the tune is naturally up tempo. Again, be careful no to let your tempo fluctuate especially since the forward roll can sometimes get ahead of you.

RIGHT-HAND PATTERN WITH CHORD EXERCISE

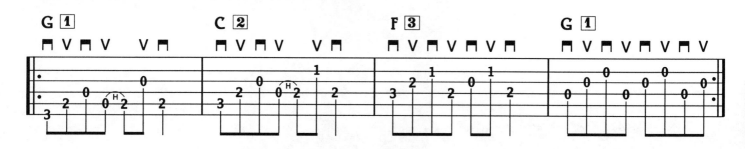

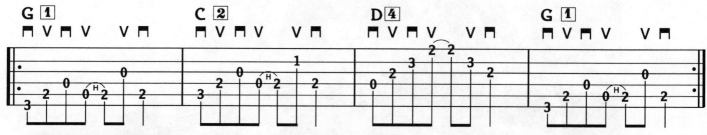

CHORD POSITIONS (Numbers in square boxes correspond to positions used in chord exercise.)

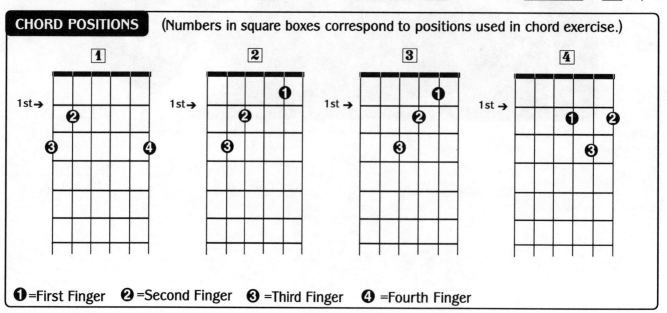

❶=First Finger   ❷=Second Finger   ❸=Third Finger   ❹=Fourth Finger

John Hardy
Preparatory Study Notes

RIGHT-HAND PATTERN

⊓ = Down Stroke
V = Up Stroke

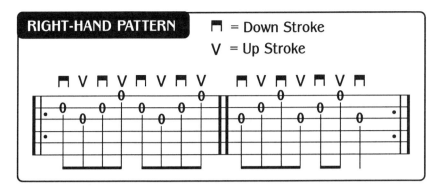

Of Noted Interest: This American ballad, about a murderer who was Afro-American named John Hardy, is now a rousing bluegrass instrumental. It's said that John Hardy himself wrote the tune awaiting his stand with the gallows pole.

RIGHT-HAND PATTERN WITH CHORD EXERCISE

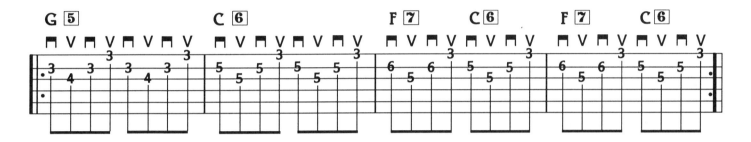

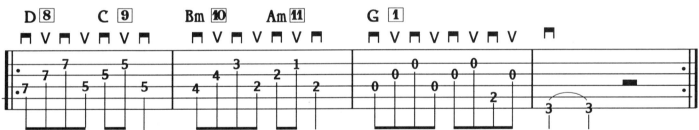

CHORD POSITIONS   (Numbers in square boxes correspond to positions used in chord exercise.)

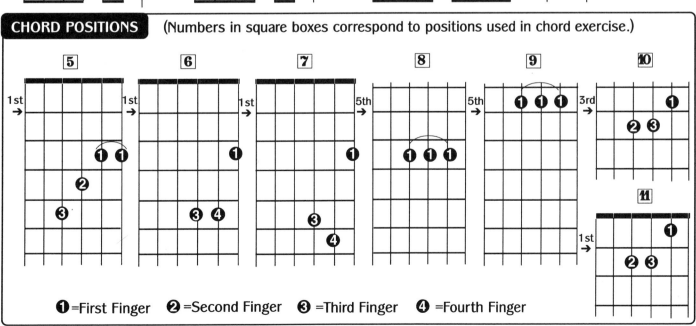

❶=First Finger   ❷=Second Finger   ❸=Third Finger   ❹=Fourth Finger

John Hardy

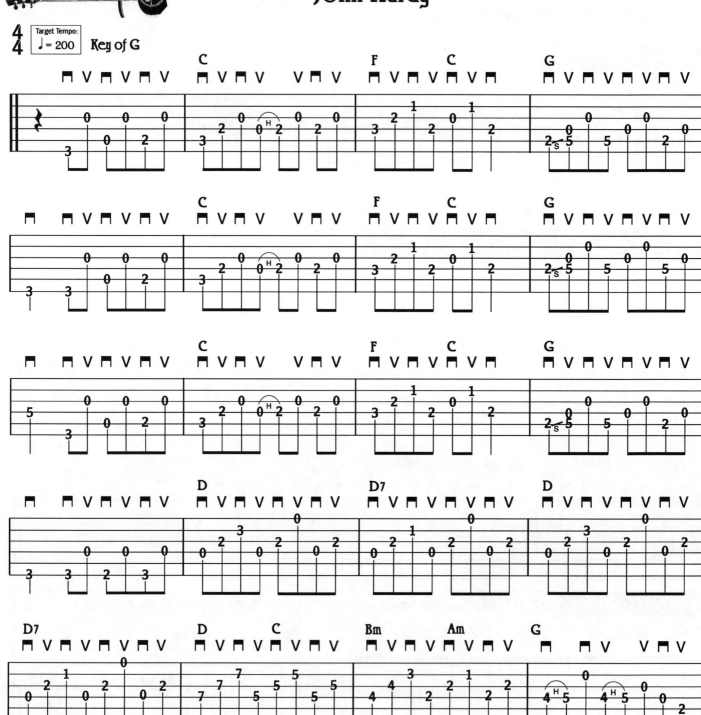

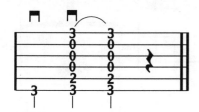

John Hardy (Variation)

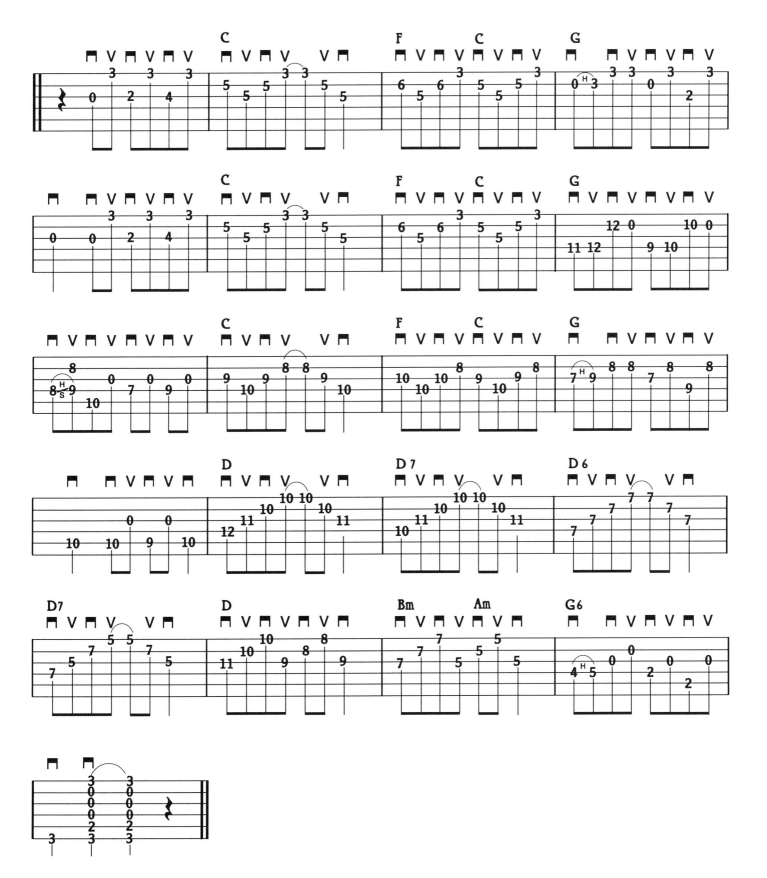

Red Wing
Preparatory Study Notes

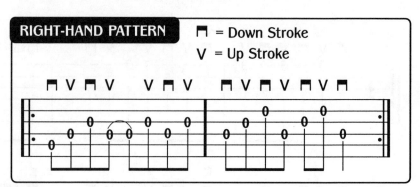

RIGHT-HAND PATTERN ⊓ = Down Stroke
V = Up Stroke

General Guidelines: The forward roll dominates this piece. Arranged to capture the feel of bluegrass banjo in "Scruggs' Style", the melody rides on the lower strings while the forward roll fills in the spaces with chordal harmonizations. Use your metronome for tempo insurance; the forward roll has a tendency to rush.

RIGHT-HAND PATTERN WITH CHORD EXERCISE

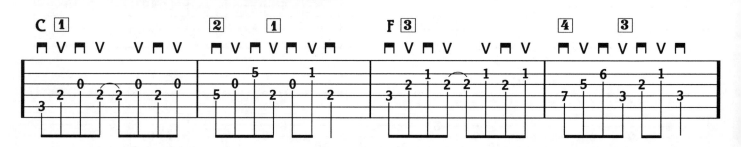

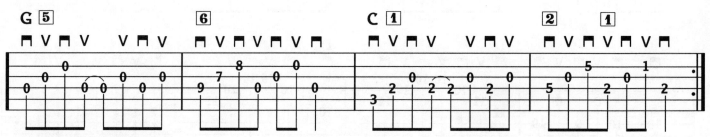

CHORD POSITIONS (Numbers in square boxes correspond to positions used in chord exercise.)

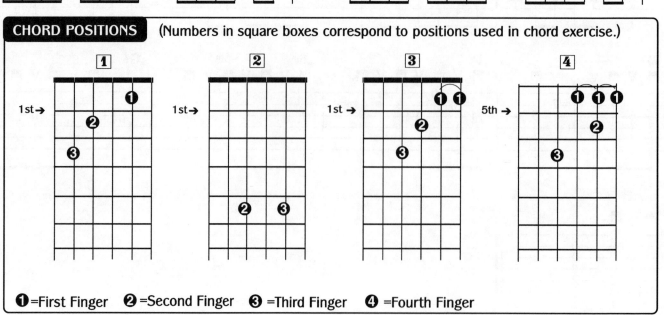

❶=First Finger   ❷=Second Finger   ❸=Third Finger   ❹=Fourth Finger

Red Wing
Preparatory Study Notes (cont.)

RIGHT-HAND PATTERN

⊓ = Down Stroke

V = Up Stroke

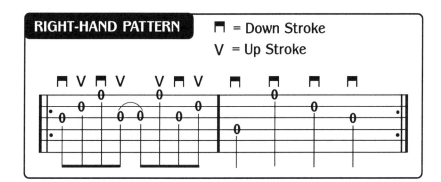

Of Noted Interest: I first learned this piece from Ray Valla's book *Deluxe Bluegrass Mandolin Method*. In fact, his influence permeates this particular guitar arrangement. If possible, listen to his arrangement first and then attempt to learn this crosspicking arrangement. You'll gain a new perspective on arranging your own crosspicking pieces and even apply the techniques to pieces you already know.

RIGHT-HAND PATTERN WITH CHORD EXERCISE

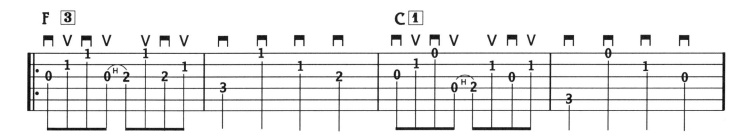

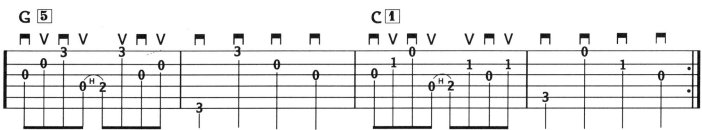

CHORD POSITIONS (Numbers in square boxes correspond to positions used in chord exercise.)

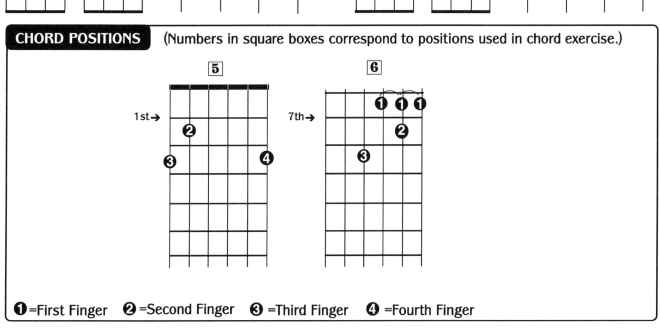

❶ =First Finger   ❷ =Second Finger   ❸ =Third Finger   ❹ =Fourth Finger

Gibson
Hummingbird
Vintage

Red Wing

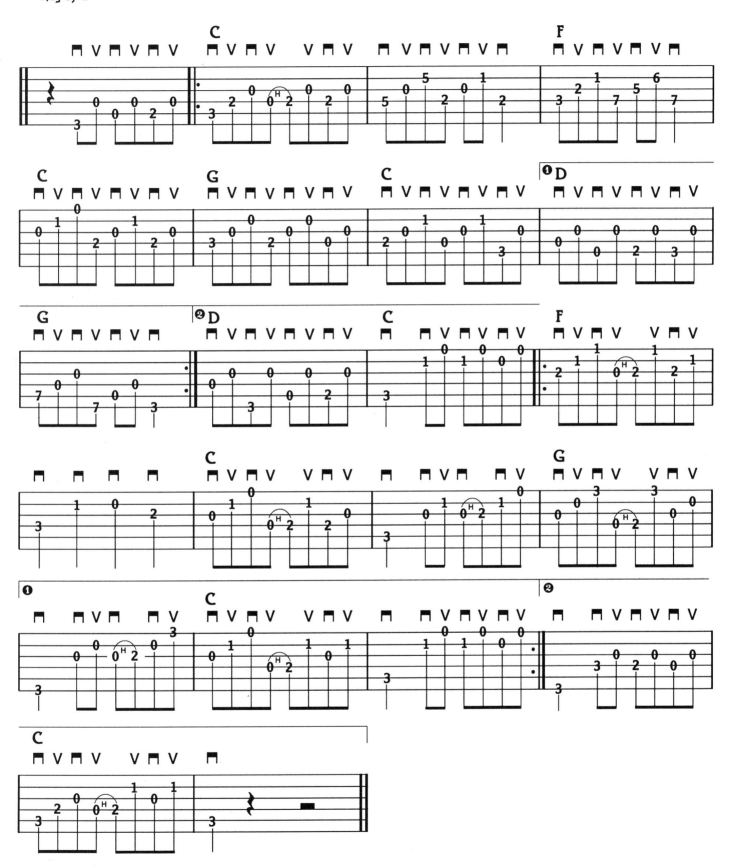

Grandfather's Clock
Preparatory Study Notes

General Guidelines: Play this tune with controlled patience. Remember, it's a song about a clock; you must not be impatient! Watch for the harmonics—they give the impression of the clock striking on the hour hand. You could also deaden the string (muting), thereby creating a "tick tock".

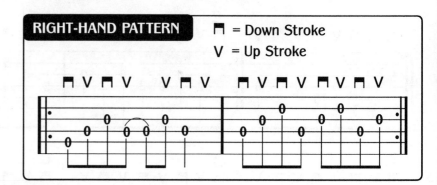

RIGHT-HAND PATTERN WITH CHORD EXERCISE

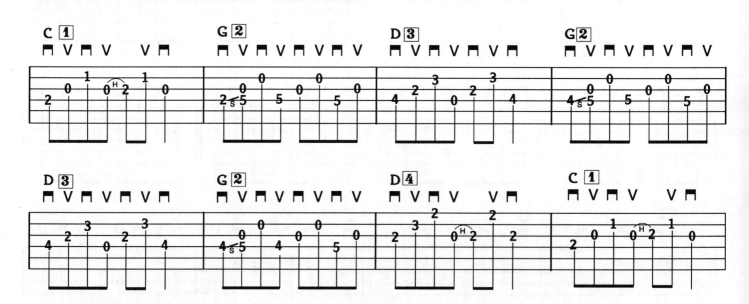

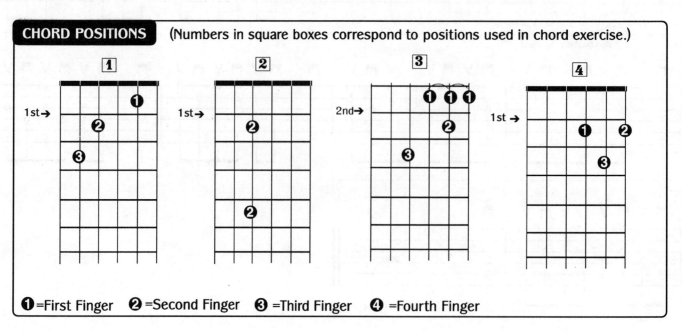

CHORD POSITIONS (Numbers in square boxes correspond to positions used in chord exercise.)

❶=First Finger   ❷=Second Finger   ❸=Third Finger   ❹=Fourth Finger

Grandfather's Clock
Preparatory Study Notes (cont.)

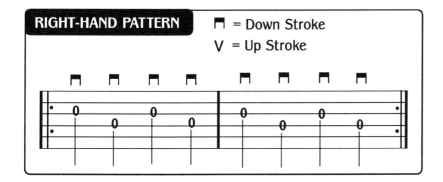

Of Noted Interest: This tune was written by Henry Work in 1876 and has undoubtedly outlived many a grandfather clock. "Grandfather's Clock" has had many arrangements created and performed on all kinds of instruments throughout its history. Yet, the one and only instrument that really breathes life into this timeless (no pun intended) piece is the banjo. Ergo, we've imitated the banjo roll on the guitar—adapting "that" banjoistic sound to the guitar for this time-honored piece.

RIGHT-HAND PATTERN WITH HARMONICS

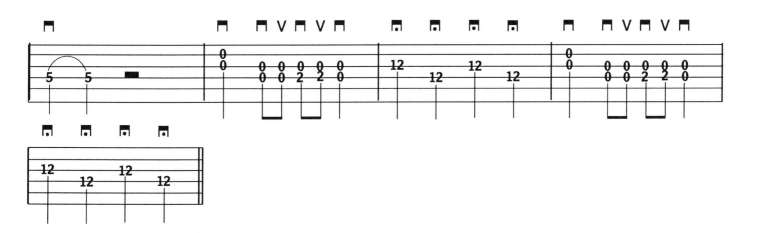

Grandfather's Clock

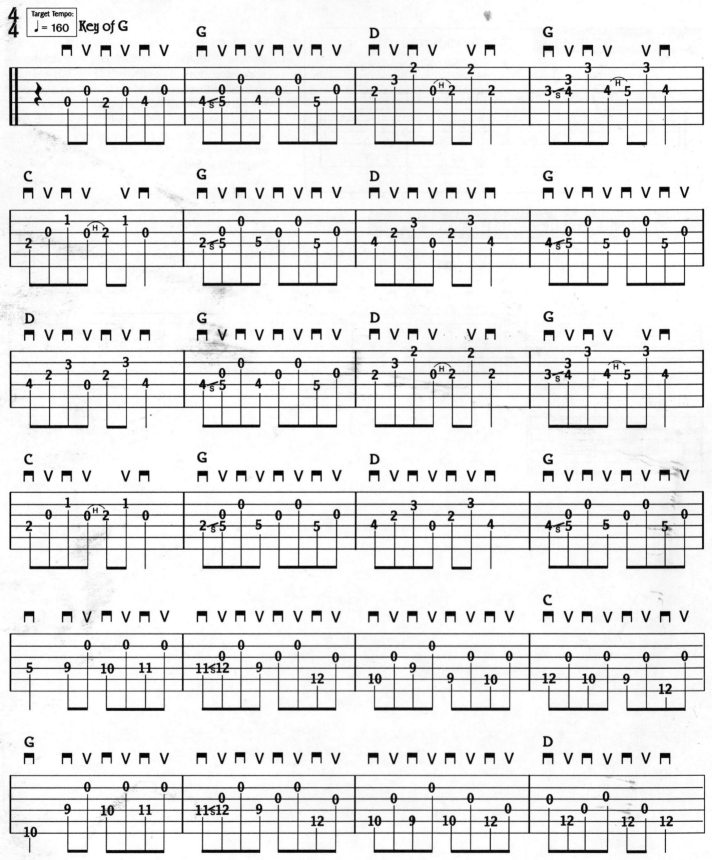

Grandfather's Clock (Continued)

Crosspicking Fiddle Style

Weave and Way

Down Yonder

Bill Cheathum

Eighth of January

Liberty

Soldier's Joy

Blackberry Blossom

Weave & Way
Preparatory Study Notes

General Guidelines: The approach to this melody is very fiddlistic in a melodic banjo sort of way. To try and capture every note of the melody, while still having the sustain of open strings to support it, was the objective. This approach can be applied effectively to all fiddle tunes. Experiment! Try adapting other fiddle tunes in the key of G utilizing some of the scales and passages illustrated in "Weave & Way".

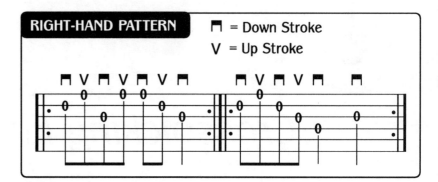

RIGHT-HAND PATTERN WITH CHORD EXERCISE

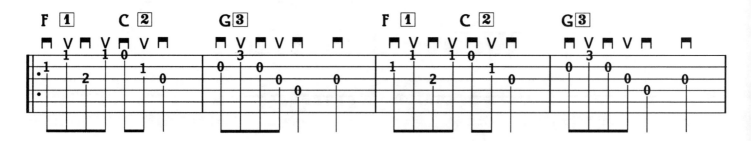

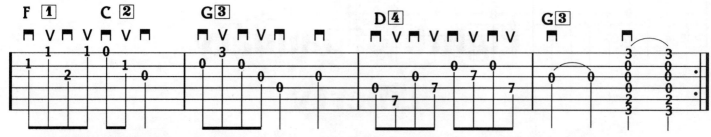

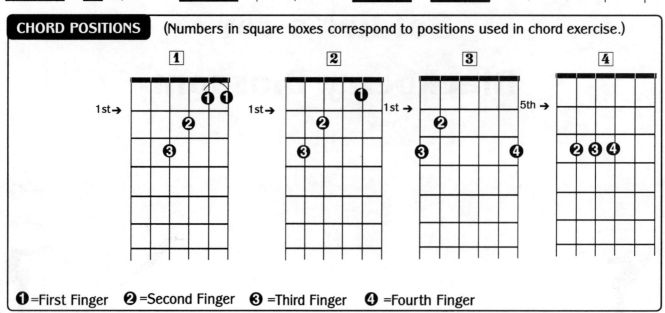

CHORD POSITIONS (Numbers in square boxes correspond to positions used in chord exercise.)

❶=First Finger ❷=Second Finger ❸=Third Finger ❹=Fourth Finger

Weave & Way
Preparatory Study Notes (cont.)

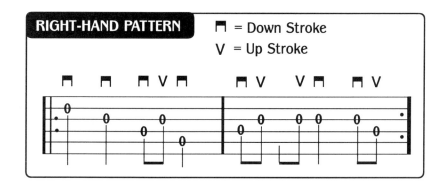

RIGHT-HAND PATTERN   ⊓ = Down Stroke
                        V = Up Stroke

Of Noted Interest: Norman Blake and Tut Taylor do a really nice version of this tune on the CD "Slow Train Through Georgia". Played as a guitar/Dobro® duet, they create some really nice texturing and harmonies. See the discography for a listing of Blake's recordings—his flatpicking guitar truly set a precedence for many aspiring acoustic guitarists.

MELODIC PASSAGES

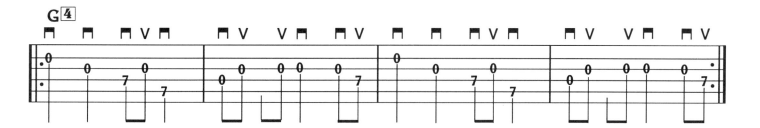

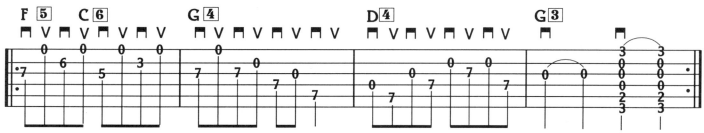

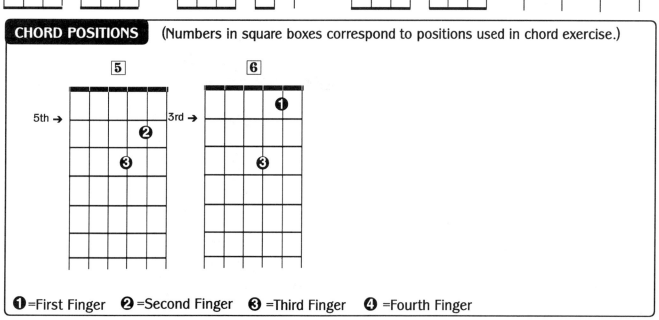

CHORD POSITIONS   (Numbers in square boxes correspond to positions used in chord exercise.)

❶=First Finger   ❷=Second Finger   ❸=Third Finger   ❹=Fourth Finger

Vintage
Martin D-18

Weave & Way

4/4
Target Tempo:
♩ = 200
Key of G

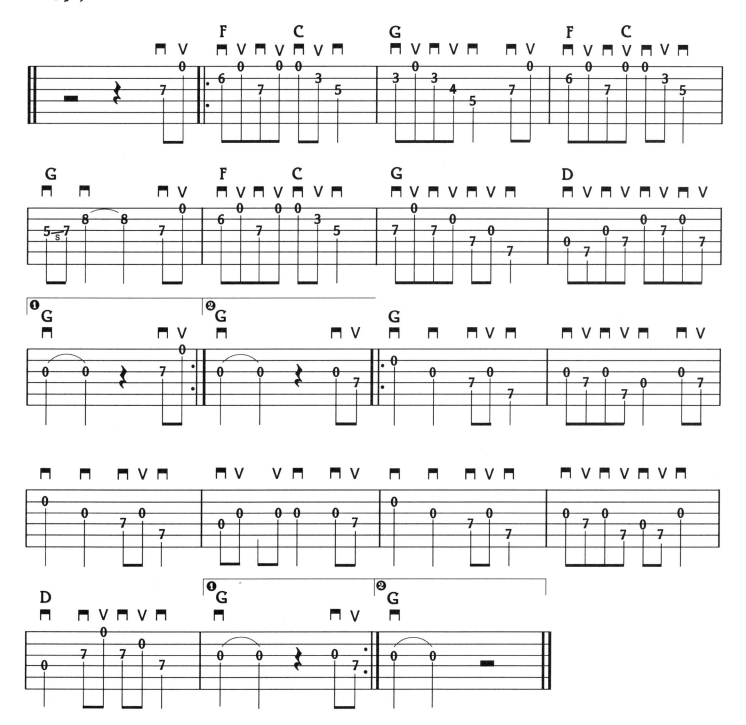

Fiddle Style

Down Yonder
Preparatory Study Notes

General Guidelines: "Down Yonder" offers some great right hand exercises. Plenty of forward rolls to continue building your dexterity for crosspicking. Watch for the simultaneous slides with the following up stroke. Pay close attention to the following exercises to ensure that you'll have this phrasing accomplished before moving on to the arrangement.

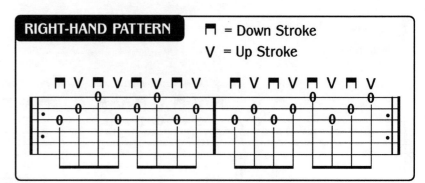

RIGHT-HAND PATTERN WITH CHORD EXERCISE

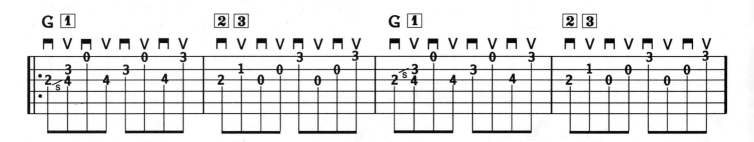

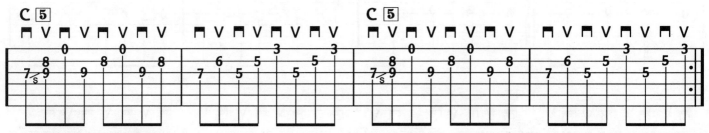

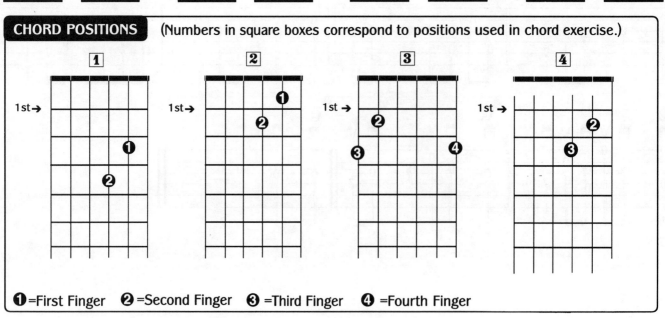

CHORD POSITIONS (Numbers in square boxes correspond to positions used in chord exercise.)

❶=First Finger ❷=Second Finger ❸=Third Finger ❹=Fourth Finger

Down Yonder
Preparatory Study Notes (cont.)

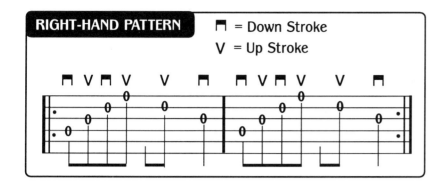

RIGHT-HAND PATTERN

⊓ = Down Stroke
V = Up Stroke

Of Noted Interest: "Down Yonder" was written by Gid Tanner and the Skillet Lickers from down Georgia way. Listen to the version on the *Will the Circle Be Unbroken* recording with the Nitty Gritty Dirt Band. It's an excellent rendition with Doc Watson leading it off with, "How does it go Vassar!"—giving the impression that it's the first take.

RIGHT-HAND PATTERN WITH CHORD EXERCISE

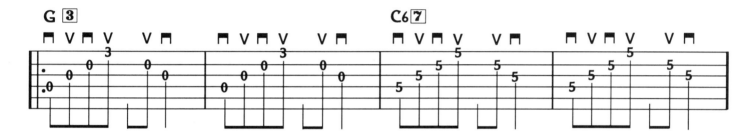

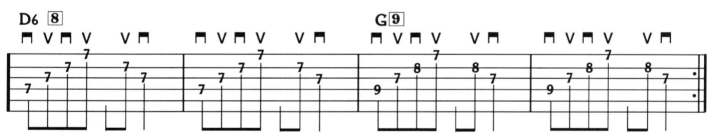

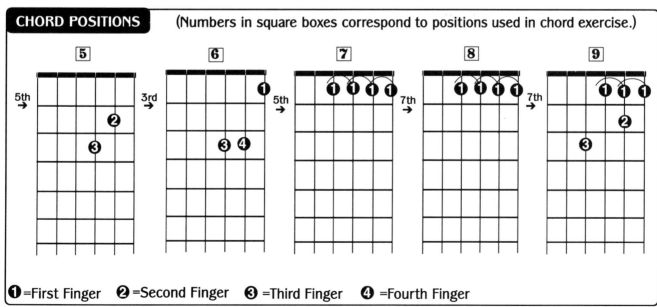

CHORD POSITIONS (Numbers in square boxes correspond to positions used in chord exercise.)

❶=First Finger ❷=Second Finger ❸=Third Finger ❹=Fourth Finger

Down Yonder

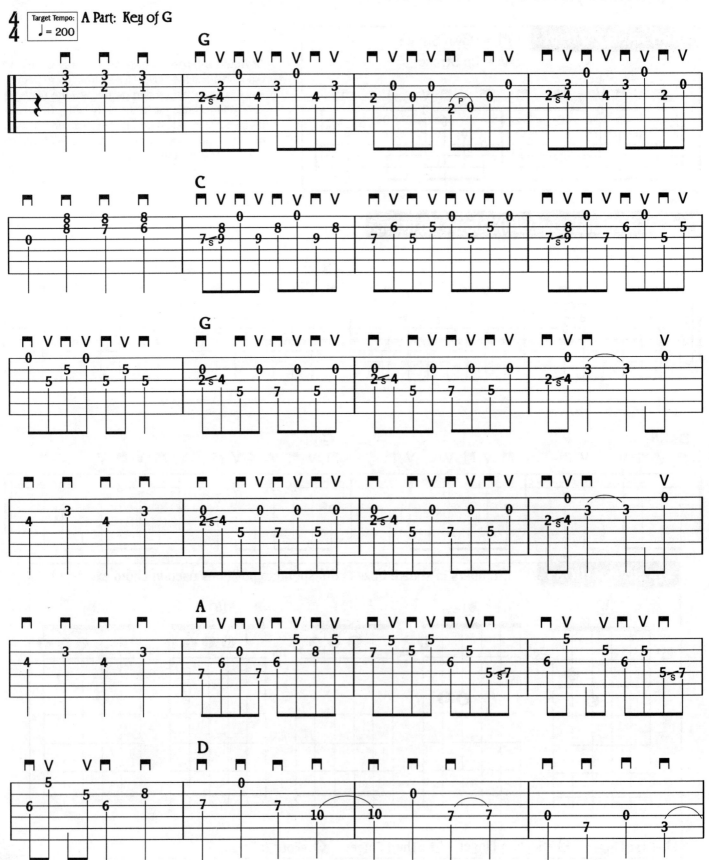

Down Yonder (Continued)

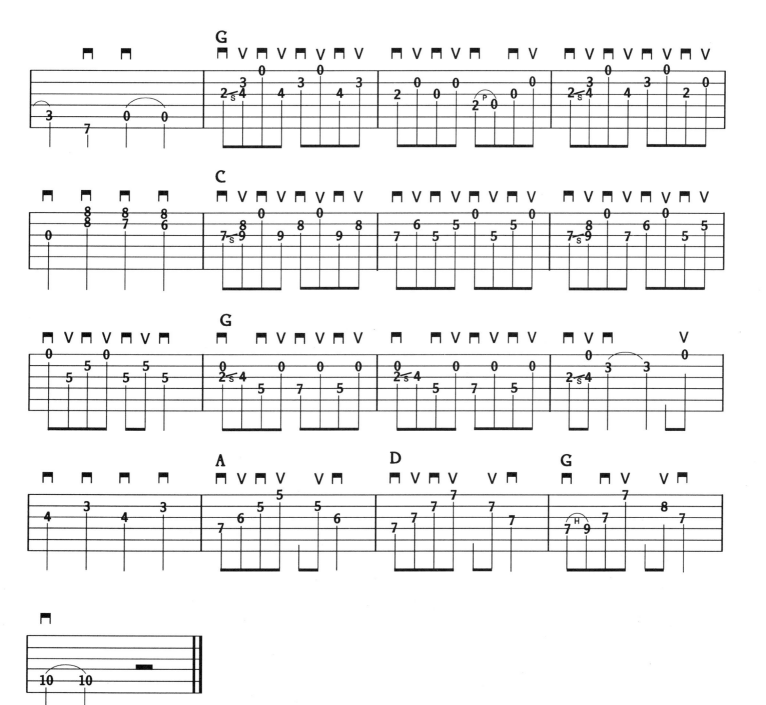

Fiddle Style

Bill Cheathum
Preparatory Study Notes

General Guidelines: This tune offers quite a bit of melodic study. Again, we're completely pulling away from chords and rolls and focusing on playing strictly melody with a crosspicking technique. Memorize these patterns and try applying them to other tunes you know in the key of G.

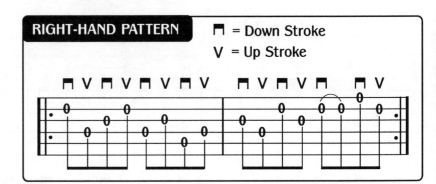

RIGHT-HAND PATTERN

⊓ = Down Stroke
V = Up Stroke

RIGHT-HAND PATTERN WITH CHORD EXERCISE

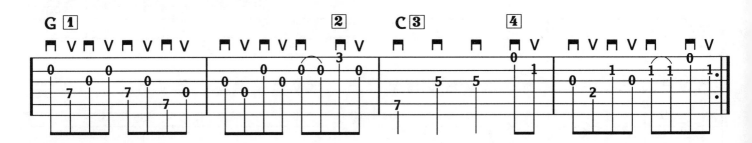

Difficult Passage

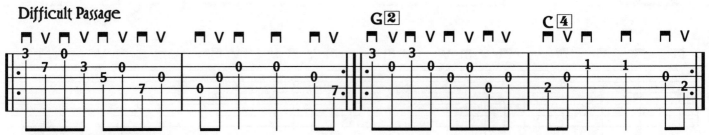

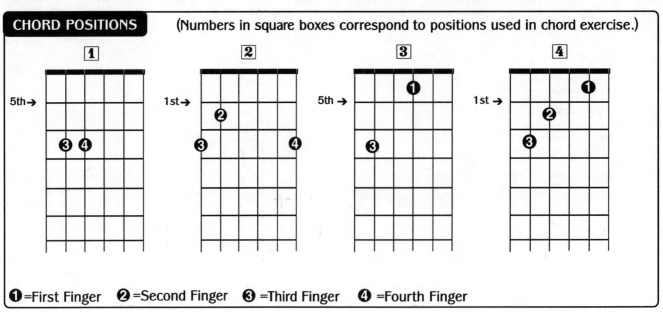

CHORD POSITIONS (Numbers in square boxes correspond to positions used in chord exercise.)

❶=First Finger   ❷=Second Finger   ❸=Third Finger   ❹=Fourth Finger

Bill Cheathum
Preparatory Study Notes (cont.)

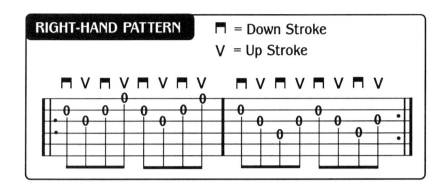

RIGHT-HAND PATTERN ⊓ = Down Stroke
V = Up Stroke

Of Noted Interest: "Bill Cheatum" is a classic fiddle tune that's been played into the ground. Here's another perspective on the tune that will change it's complexion and vary your breaks. Start off with the standard flatpicking approach and then break into this arrangement on your following take.

RIGHT-HAND PATTERN WITH CHORD EXERCISE

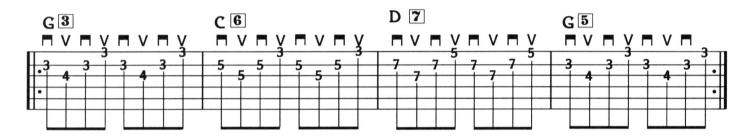

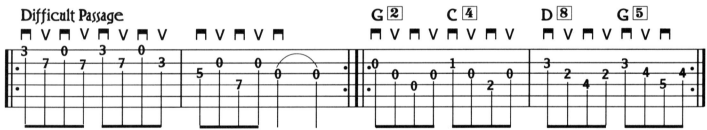

CHORD POSITIONS (Numbers in square boxes correspond to positions used in chord exercise.)

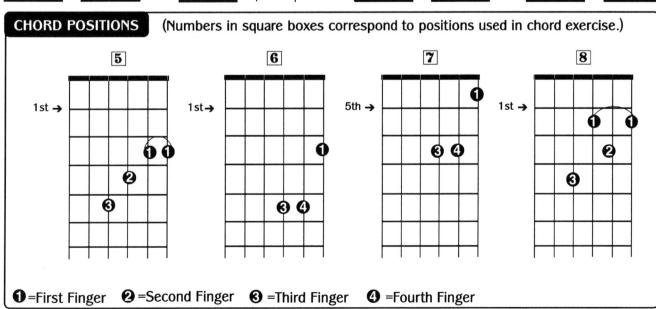

❶=First Finger ❷=Second Finger ❸=Third Finger ❹=Fourth Finger

Bill Cheathum

4/4 Target Tempo: ♩ = 185
Key of G

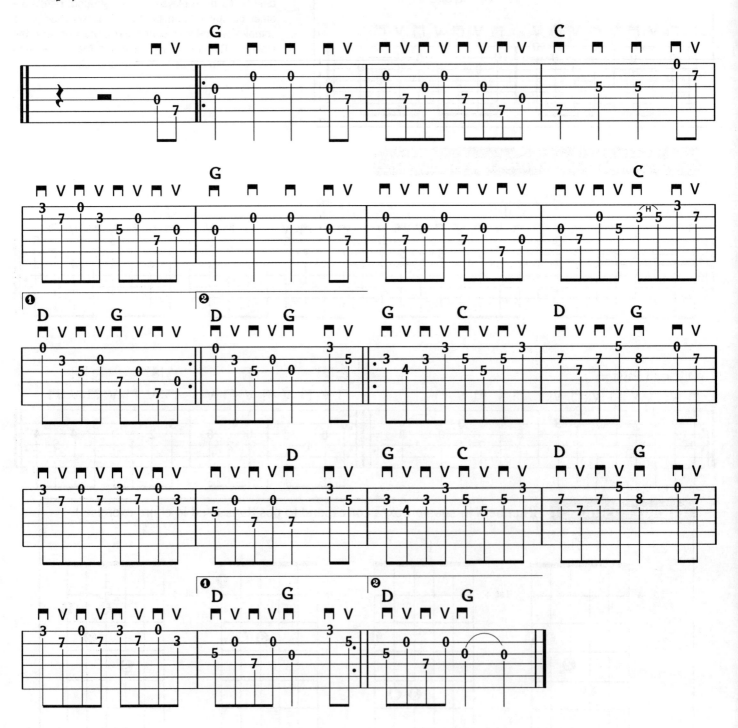

Fiddle Style

Vintage
Gibson
Hummingbird
Lefty Model

Eighth of January
Preparatory Study Notes (cont.)

General Guidelines: The approach to this melody is very fiddlistic in a melodic banjo sort of way. To try and capture every note of the melody, while still having the sustain of open strings to support it, was the objective. This approach can be applied effectively to all fiddle tunes. Experiment! Try adapting other fiddle tunes in the key of C and G utilizing some of the scales and passages illustrated in "Eighth of January".

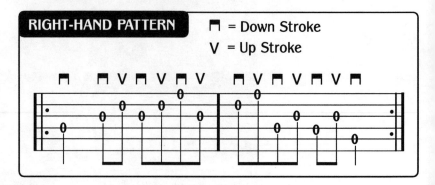

RIGHT-HAND PATTERN   ⊓ = Down Stroke   V = Up Stroke

RIGHT-HAND PATTERN WITH CHORD EXERCISE

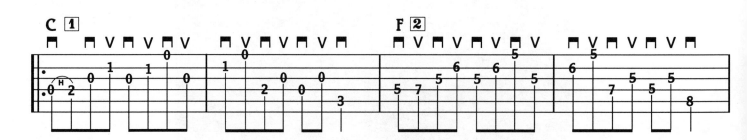

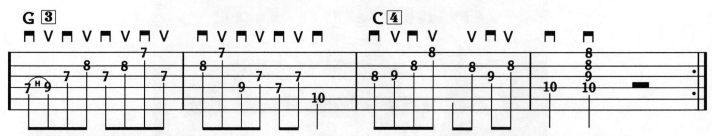

CHORD POSITIONS   (Numbers in square boxes correspond to positions used in chord exercise.)

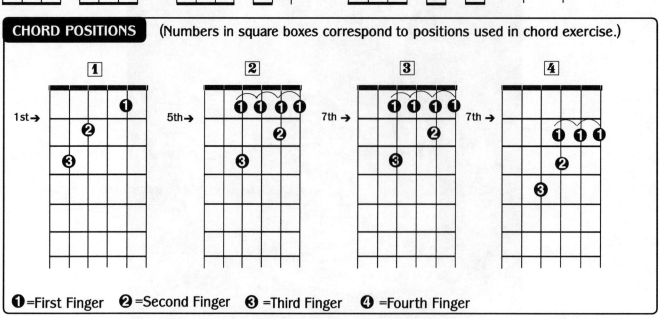

❶ =First Finger   ❷ =Second Finger   ❸ =Third Finger   ❹ =Fourth Finger

Eighth of January
Preparatory Study Notes (cont.)

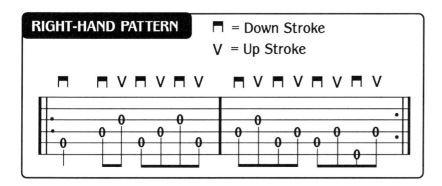

RIGHT-HAND PATTERN   ⊓ = Down Stroke
                          V = Up Stroke

Of Noted Interest: Jimmy Driftwood had originally incorporated this melody into his famous composition "The Battle of New Orleans". The tune was written originally by frontier fiddlers in commemoration of the battle that took place in 1814. Because of Driftwood's songwriting efforts, everyone is familiar with this melody today.

RIGHT-HAND PATTERN WITH CHORD EXERCISE

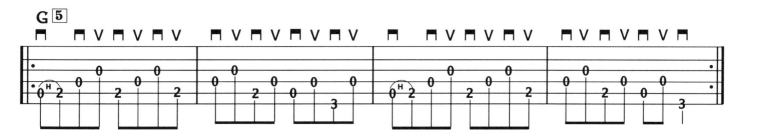

C Scale Exercise   ### G Scale Exercise

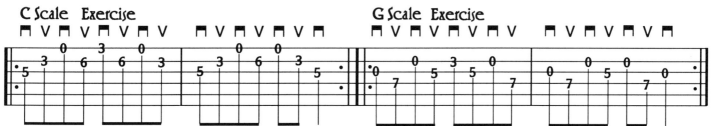

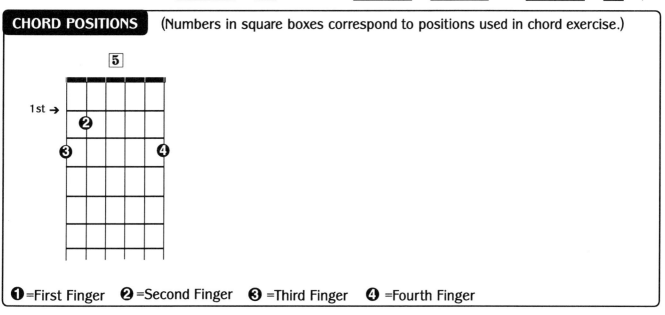

CHORD POSITIONS   (Numbers in square boxes correspond to positions used in chord exercise.)

❶=First Finger   ❷=Second Finger   ❸=Third Finger   ❹=Fourth Finger

Fiddle Style

Eighth Of January

4/4 Target Tempo: ♩ = 175

Key of C

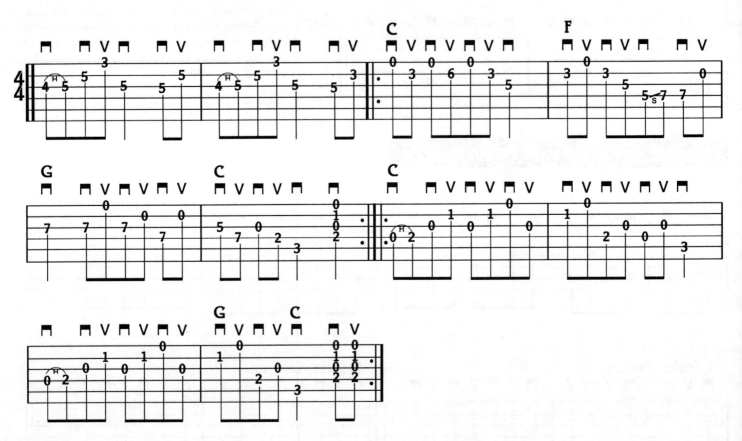

Eighth Of January (Variation)

Target Tempo:
♩ = 175

Key of G

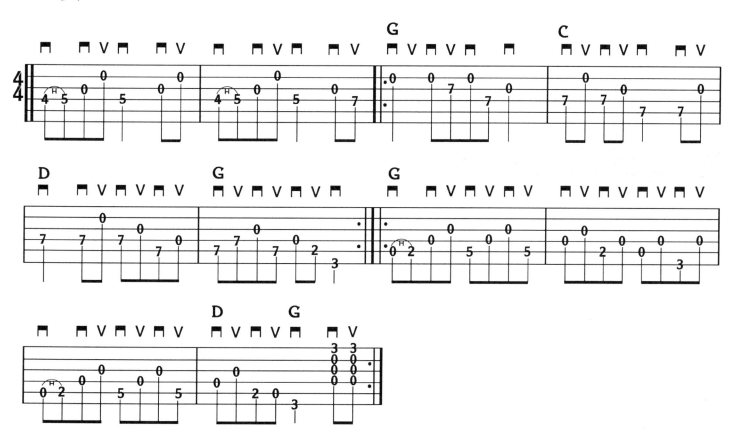

Liberty
Preparatory Study Notes

General Guidelines: Here we will be concentrating on forward/reverse rolls...another great dexterity builder for the flatpicking hand.

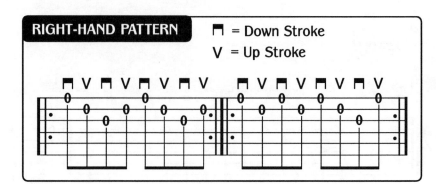

RIGHT-HAND PATTERN WITH CHORD EXERCISE

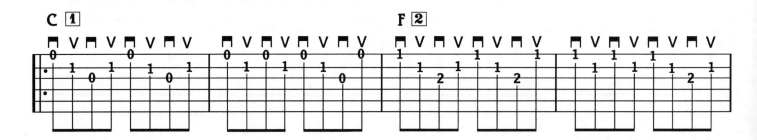

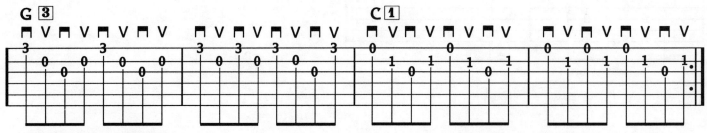

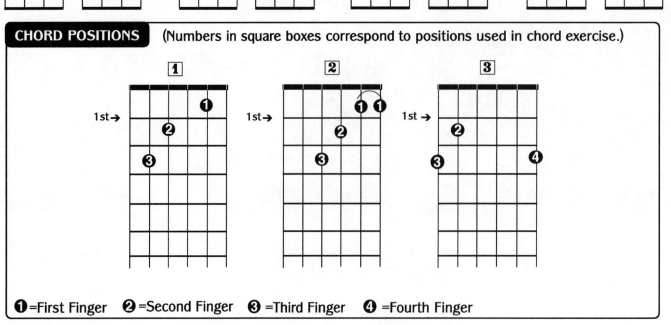

CHORD POSITIONS (Numbers in square boxes correspond to positions used in chord exercise.)

❶=First Finger ❷=Second Finger ❸=Third Finger ❹=Fourth Finger

Fiddle Style

Liberty
Preparatory Study Notes (cont.)

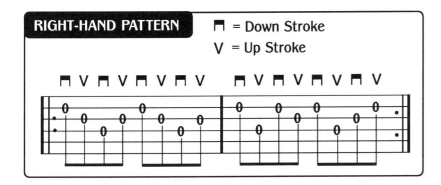

RIGHT-HAND PATTERN

⊓ = Down Stroke
V = Up Stroke

Of Noted Interest: Here's another classic fiddle tune that every parking lot picker should know. It probably dates back to post colonial times when freedom wasn't taken for granted. The title "Liberty" is a word seldom celebrated as it really should be!

RIGHT-HAND PATTERN WITH CHORD EXERCISE

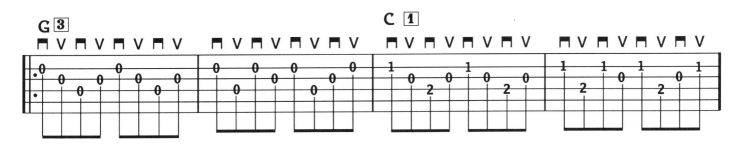

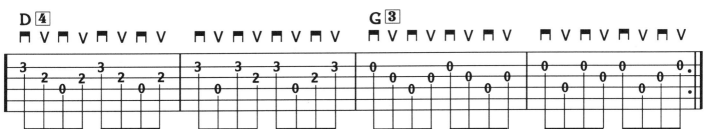

CHORD POSITIONS (Numbers in square boxes correspond to positions used in chord exercise.)

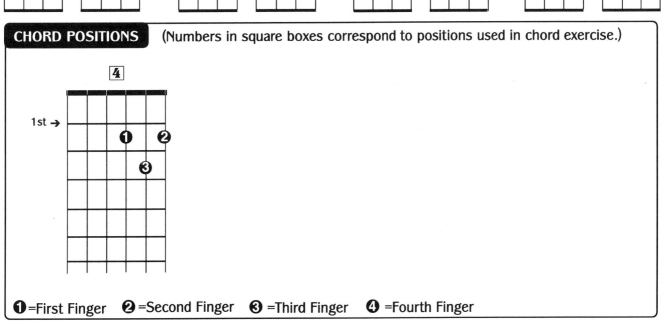

❶=First Finger   ❷=Second Finger   ❸=Third Finger   ❹=Fourth Finger

Fiddle Style

Liberty

4/4 Target Tempo: ♩ = 200

Key of C

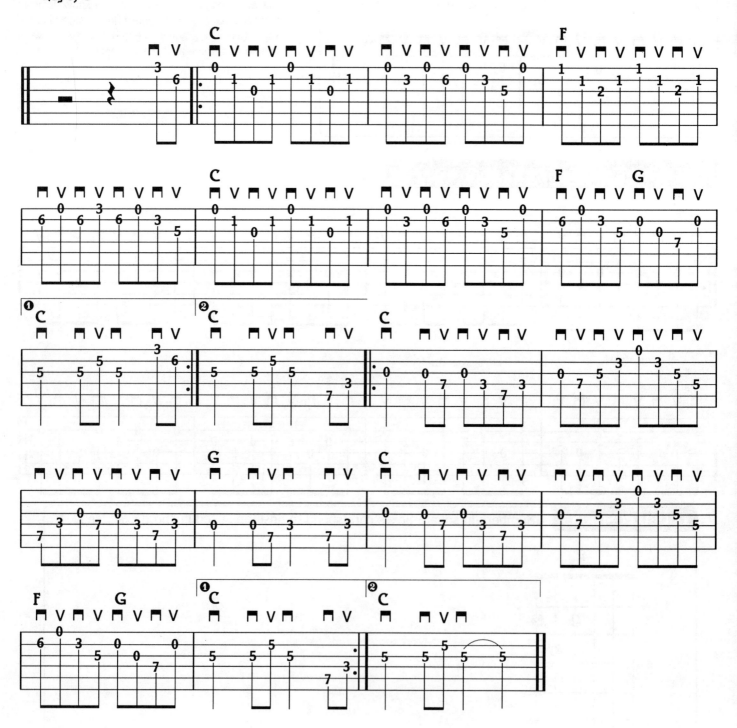

Liberty (Variation)

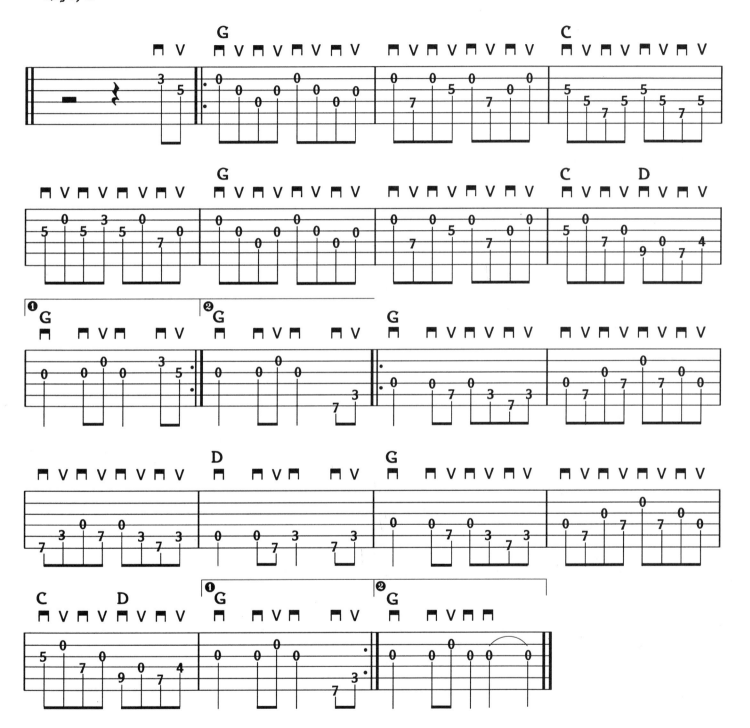

Soldier's Joy
Preparatory Study Notes

General Guidelines: Think frailing banjo when playing this arrangement. Notice particularly the droning "D" open string. Be careful not to mute it when fretting adjacent strings. This drone is what flavors the tune similar to a frailing banjo. Focus on the difficult passage sections to ensure that you don't have any bottlenecks.

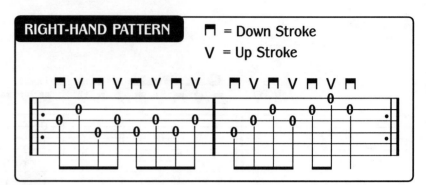

RIGHT-HAND PATTERN WITH CHORD EXERCISE

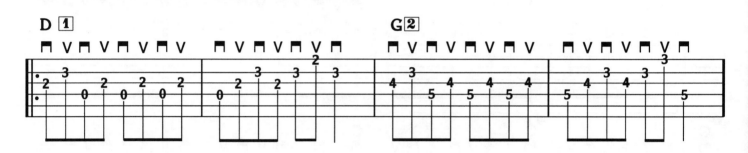

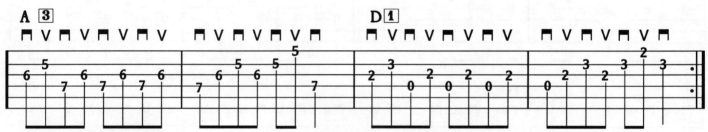

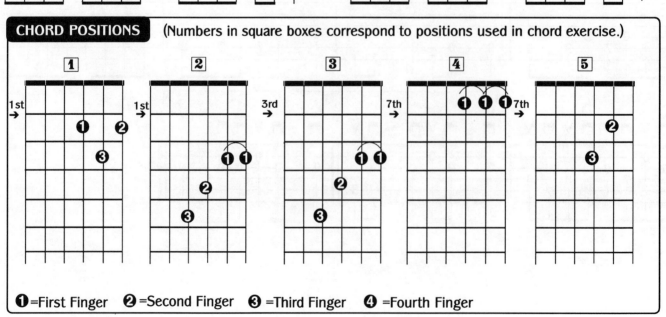

CHORD POSITIONS (Numbers in square boxes correspond to positions used in chord exercise.)

❶=First Finger ❷=Second Finger ❸=Third Finger ❹=Fourth Finger

Soldier's Joy
Preparatory Study Notes (cont.)

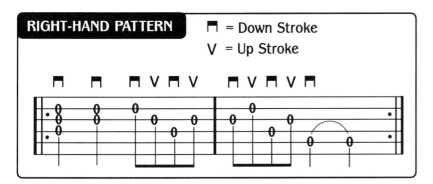

RIGHT-HAND PATTERN

⊓ = Down Stroke

V = Up Stroke

General Guidelines: One of my favorite versions of this tune is on the Nitty Gritty Dirt Band production *Will the Circle Be Unbroken* as a banjo duet with string bass backup. The following arrangement possesses similar overtones and sounds great unaccompanied.

RIGHT-HAND PATTERN WITH CHORD EXERCISE

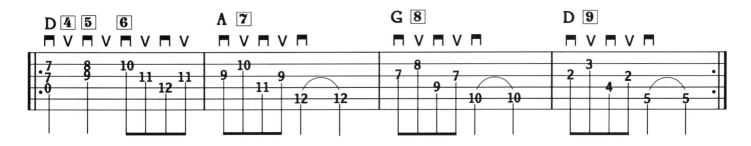

Difficult Passage

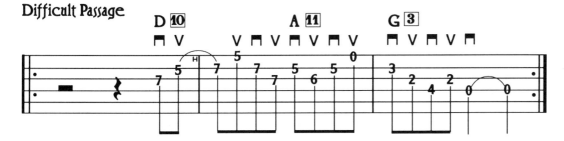

CHORD POSITIONS (Numbers in square boxes correspond to positions used in chord exercise.)

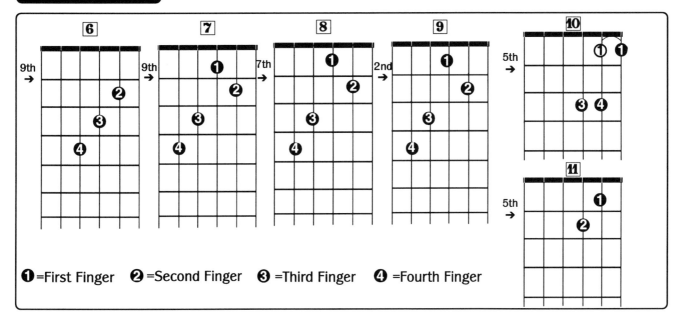

❶=First Finger ❷=Second Finger ❸=Third Finger ❹=Fourth Finger

Solder's Joy

$\frac{4}{4}$ Target Tempo: ♩ = 180

Key of D

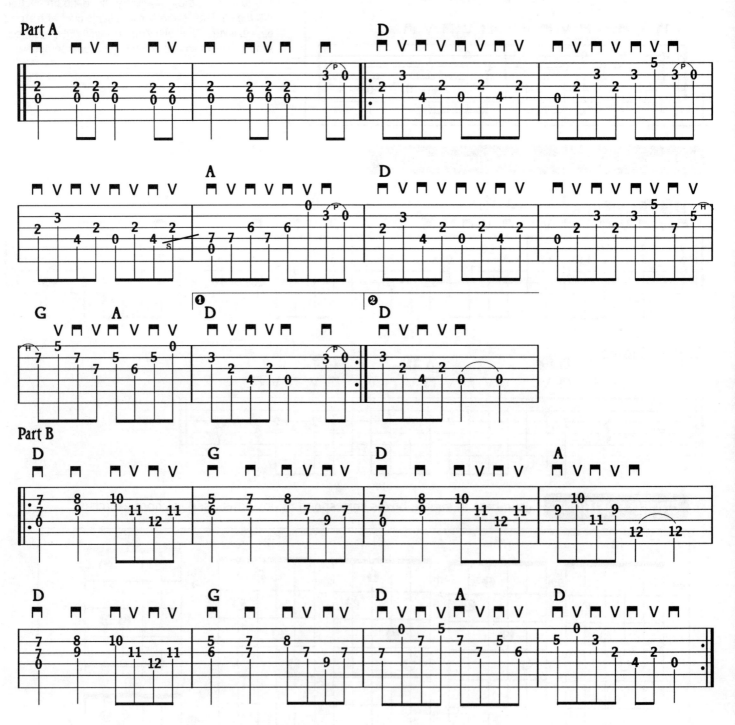

Solder's Joy (Continued)

Page 79.

Ending

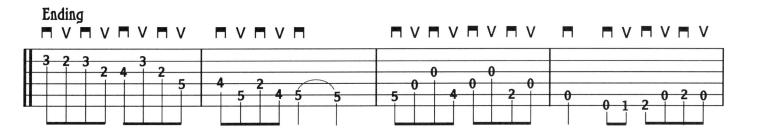

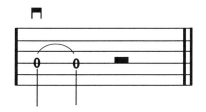

Fiddle Style

Blackberry Blossom
Preparatory Study Notes

General Guidelines: Blackberry Blossom is normally played fast in a bluegrass setting. It happens to be a beautiful melody played fast or slow. This arrangement lends itself to be played at a medium pace. (Metronome Setting 190) This tune does require some rapid chord changes. Before attempting the exercises, try strumming the chords out at two beats per chord. This will establish left hand facility before trying to employ the intricacies of the crosspicking patterns.

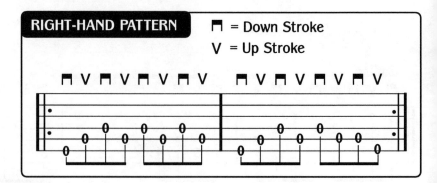

RIGHT-HAND PATTERN WITH CHORD EXERCISE

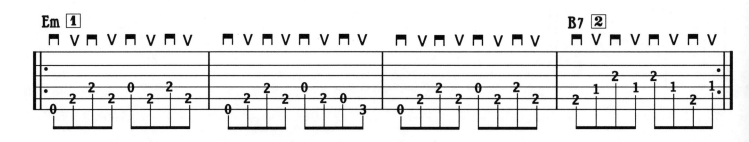

G Scale Exercise

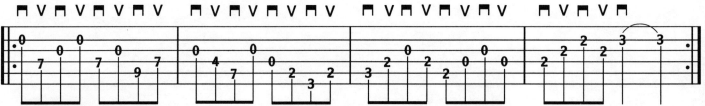

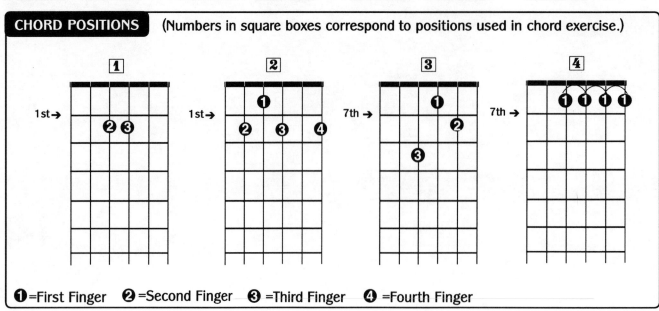

❶=First Finger ❷=Second Finger ❸=Third Finger ❹=Fourth Finger

Blackberry Blossom
Preparatory Study Notes (cont.)

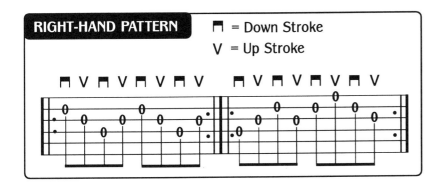

RIGHT-HAND PATTERN   ⊓ = Down Stroke
V = Up Stroke

Of Noted Interest: Even though it originated as a fiddle tune, this melody seems to have been written with melodic banjo in mind. Alan Munde does a great rendition of this on his tour de force *Banjo Sandwich.*

RIGHT-HAND PATTERN WITH CHORD EXERCISE

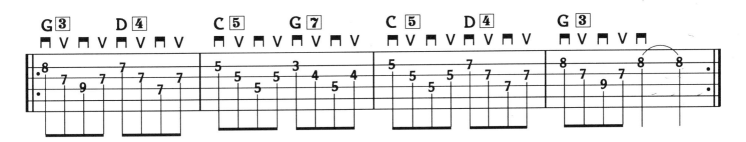

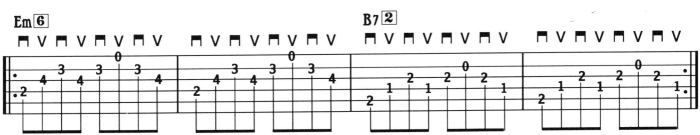

CHORD POSITIONS   (Numbers in square boxes correspond to positions used in chord exercise.)

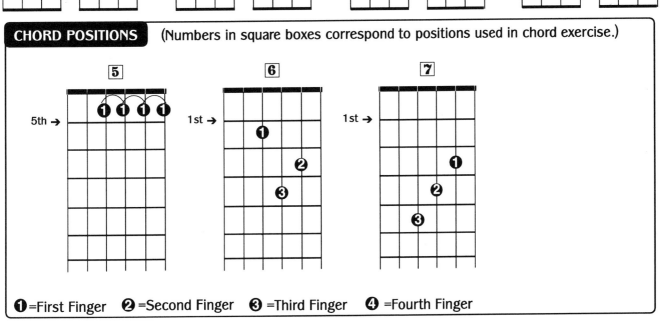

❶=First Finger   ❷=Second Finger   ❸=Third Finger   ❹=Fourth Finger

Fiddle Style

Blackberry Blossom (Variation 1)

$\frac{4}{4}$ **Target Tempo:** ♩ = 190
Key of G

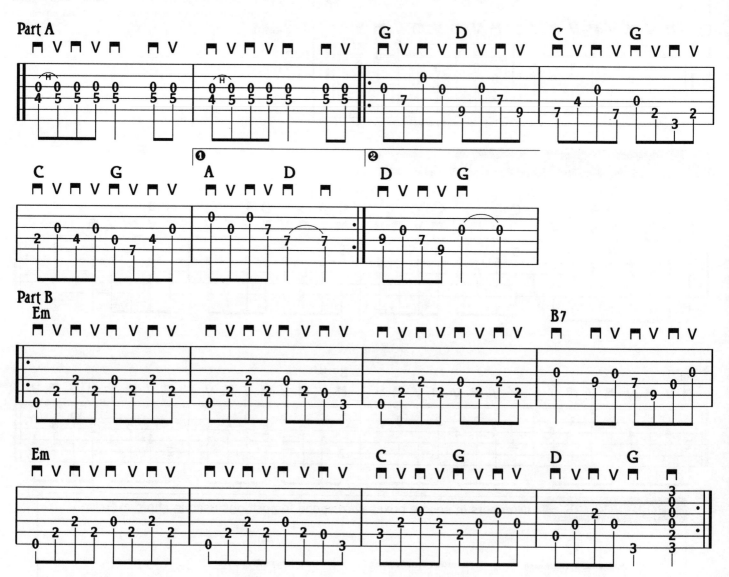

Fiddle Style

Blackberry Blossom (Variaton 2)

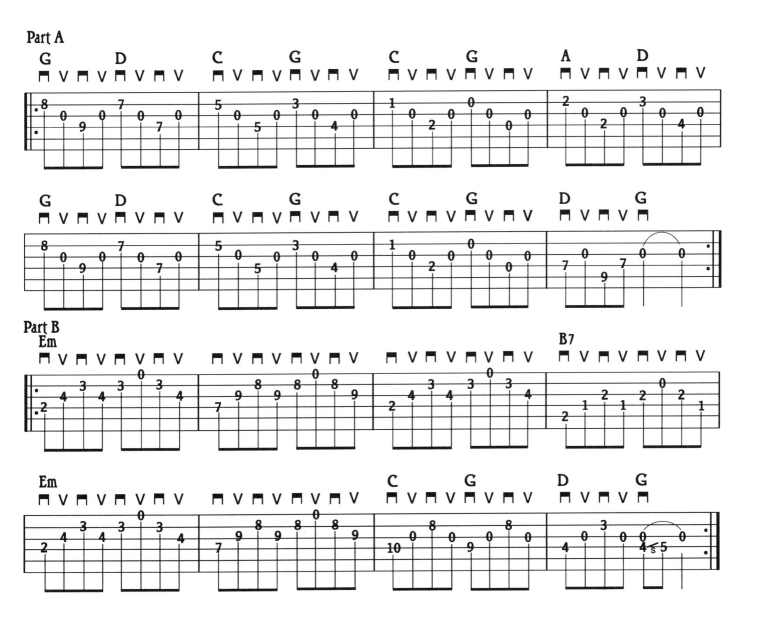

Taylor
Cutaway

Crosspicking Classical Style

Greensleeves

Ode to Joy

Malagueña

Greensleeves
Preparatory Study Notes

General Guidelines: This melody is normally played in 3/4 time. Our arrangement, adapted to crosspicking, is written in 4/4 time and is played slightly faster than what is expected. As a variation, try playing this melody slowly in 3/4 time and then jumping into the 4/4 crosspicking arrangement. It will add the surprise element to your performance and may even keep your audience from nodding off.

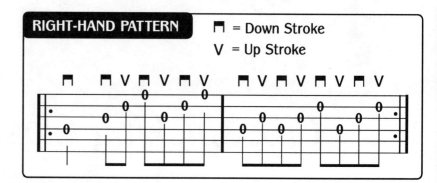

RIGHT-HAND PATTERN WITH CHORD EXERCISE

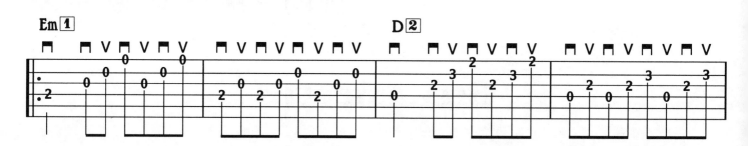

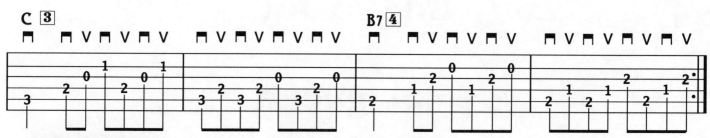

CHORD POSITIONS (Numbers in square boxes correspond to positions used in chord exercise.)

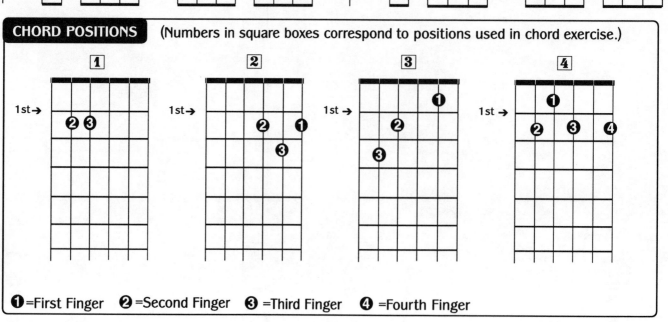

❶=First Finger ❷=Second Finger ❸=Third Finger ❹=Fourth Finger

Classical Style

Greensleeves
Preparatory Study Notes (cont.)

Of Noted Interest: This melody has been ascribed to King Henry the VIII–no doubt, it's centuries old yet, nonetheless, defeats time.

RIGHT-HAND PATTERN

⊓ = Down Stroke

V = Up Stroke

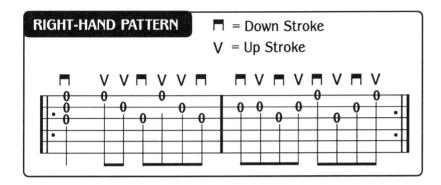

RIGHT-HAND PATTERN WITH CHORD EXERCISE

G 5   D 2

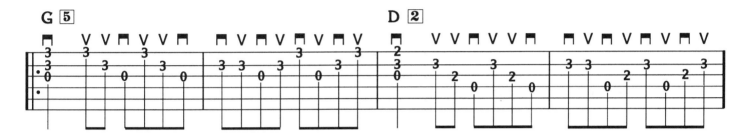

C 3   B7 4

CHORD POSITIONS (Numbers in square boxes correspond to positions used in chord exercise.)

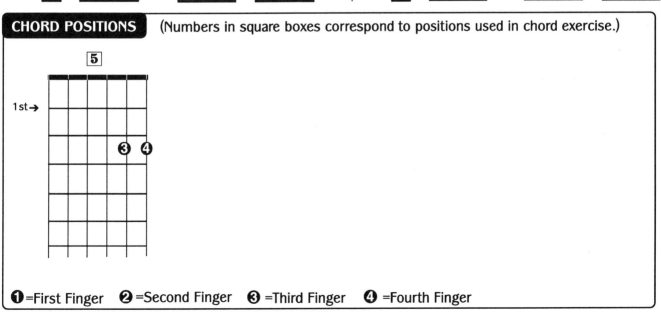

❶=First Finger   ❷=Second Finger   ❸=Third Finger   ❹=Fourth Finger

Classical Style

Greensleeves

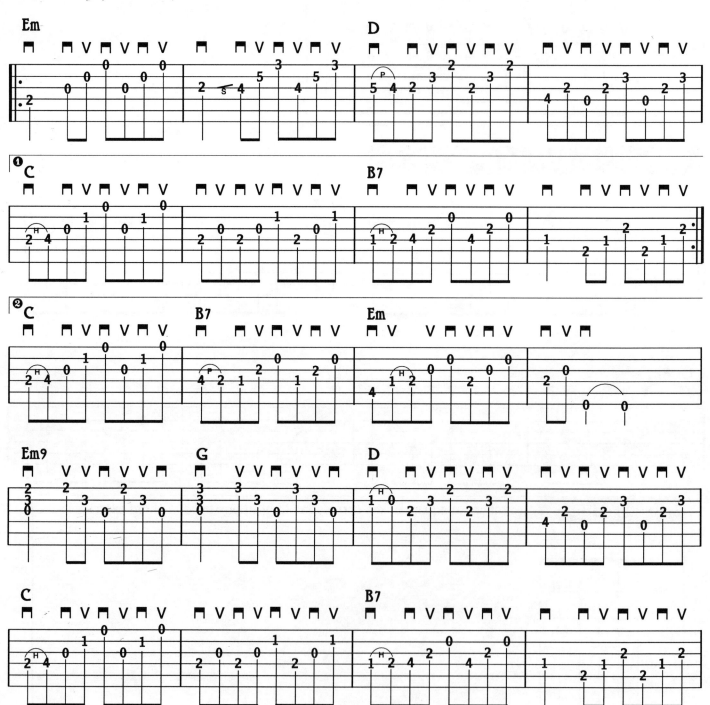

Greensleeves (Continued)

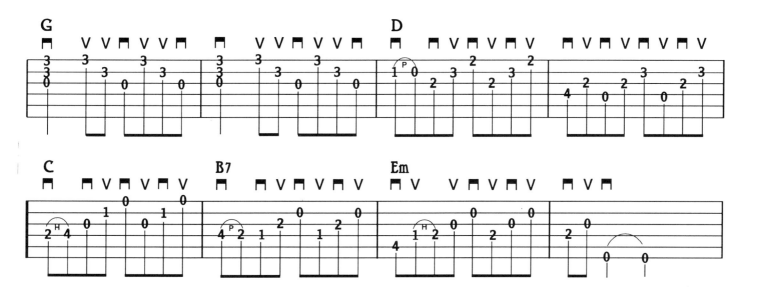

Classical Style

Ode To Joy
Preparatory Study Notes

General Guidelines: In this arrangement, drone notes are being played throughout the piece. The crosspicking pattern follows the alternating bass variation. You may vary your accents by placing them on either the melody notes or the drone notes. This piece makes for an excellent flatpicking hand workout.

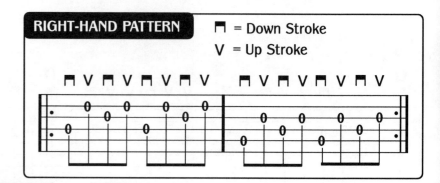

RIGHT-HAND PATTERN WITH CHORD EXERCISE

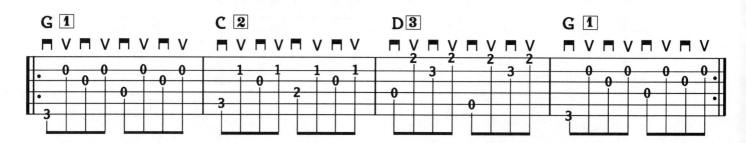

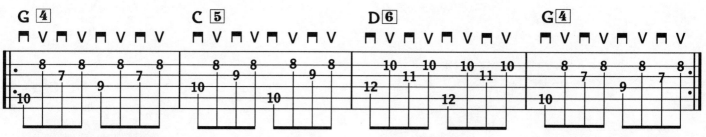

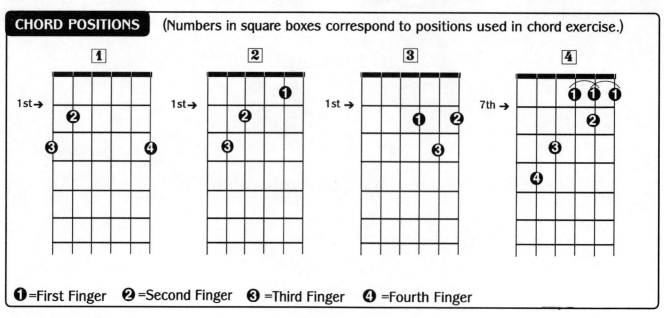

CHORD POSITIONS (Numbers in square boxes correspond to positions used in chord exercise.)

❶ =First Finger   ❷ =Second Finger   ❸ =Third Finger   ❹ =Fourth Finger

Classical Style

Ode To Joy
Preparatory Study Notes

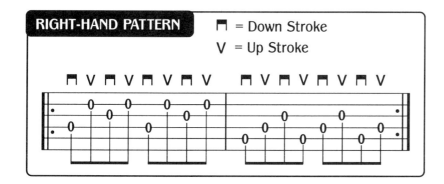

RIGHT-HAND PATTERN   ⊓ = Down Stroke
                 V = Up Stroke

Of Noted Interest: Also known as "Beethoven's Ninth", or "Beethoven's Chorale", this interpretation has a very improvisatory feel. Timing is not critical; you may speed it up or slow it down in parts without sacrificing the mood of the piece. The melody is simple but persuasive.

RIGHT-HAND PATTERN WITH CHORD EXERCISE

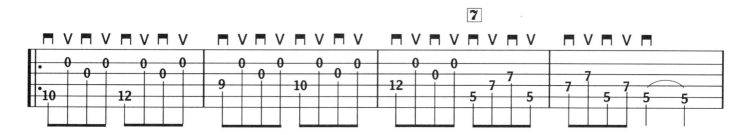

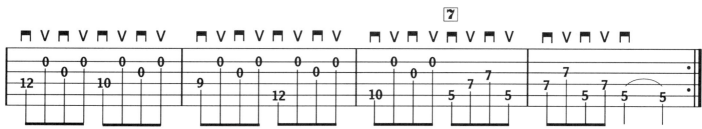

CHORD POSITIONS   (Numbers in square boxes correspond to positions used in chord exercise.)

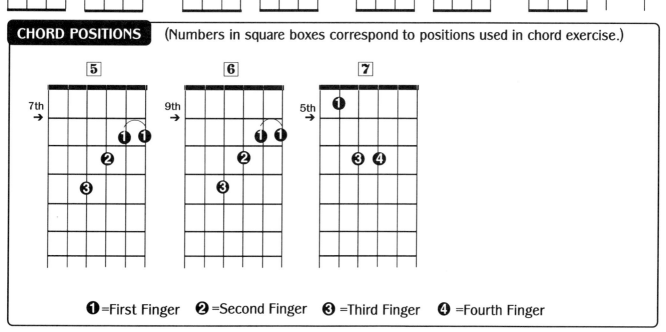

❶ =First Finger   ❷ =Second Finger   ❸ =Third Finger   ❹ =Fourth Finger

Ode To Joy

(Beethoven)

4/4 Target Tempo: ♩ = 170

Key of G

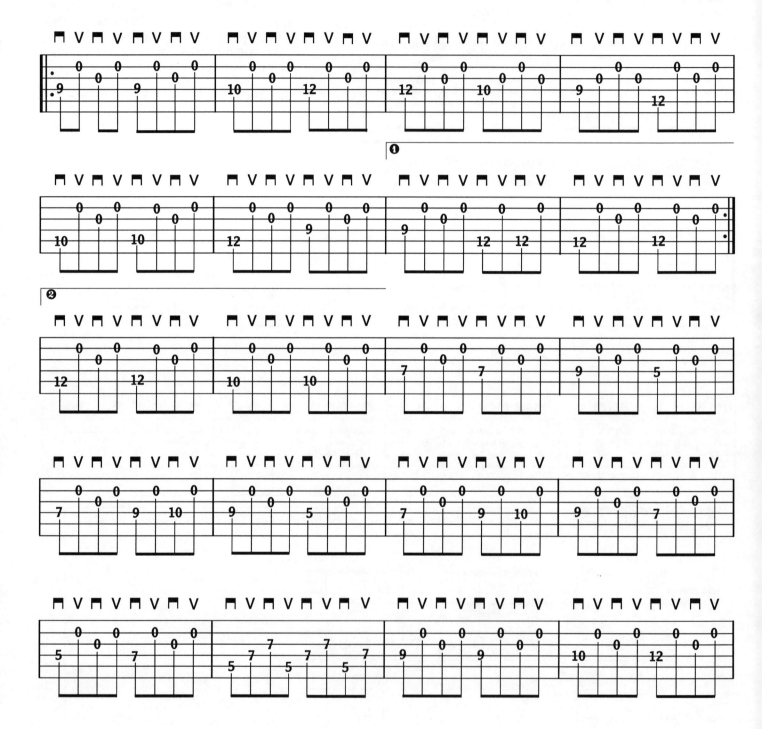

Classical Style

Ode To Joy (Continued)

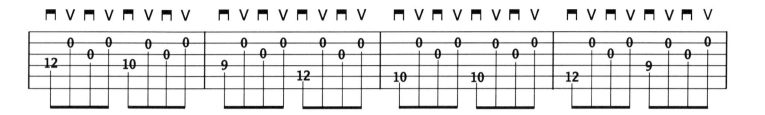

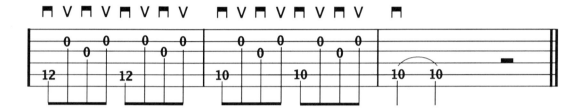

Classical Style

Malagueña
Preparatory Study Notes

General Guidelines: When attempting this arrangement, start the tune off slowly on the first time around. The final repeat of the tune should be at the target tempo of 180 on the metronome. The most difficult part of this piece involves the span that the flatpicking hand must make to jump from the third string to the first string—if accomplished properly, you should sound like you're fingerpicking instead of flatpicking.

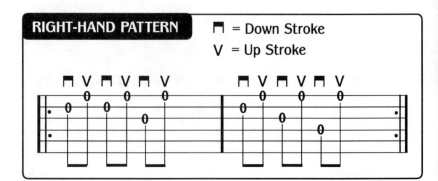

RIGHT-HAND PATTERN WITH CHORD EXERCISE

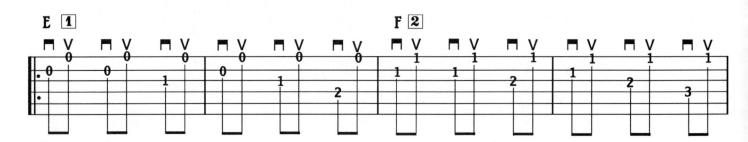

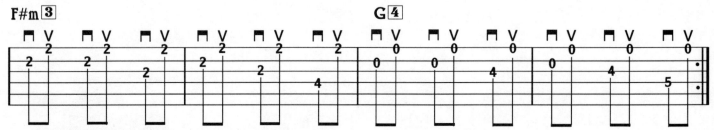

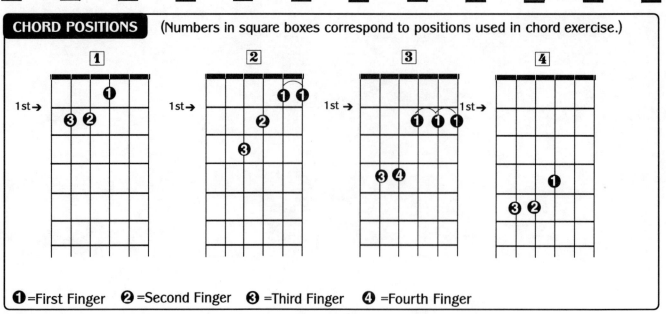

CHORD POSITIONS (Numbers in square boxes correspond to positions used in chord exercise.)

❶=First Finger   ❷=Second Finger   ❸=Third Finger   ❹=Fourth Finger

Malagueña
Preparatory Study Notes

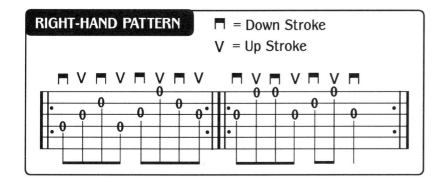

RIGHT-HAND PATTERN ⊓ = Down Stroke V = Up Stroke

Of Noted Interest: You've heard flamenco fingestyle guitar–now we have flamenco flatpicking guitar. Malagueña is in triple-time based on a dance from Malaga Spain. This tune just touches on the many possibilities crosspicking offers in a flamenco vein. A couple of guitarists that expounded on this flatpicking flamenco include: Dan Crary and Al Dimeola.

RIGHT-HAND PATTERN WITH CHORD EXERCISE

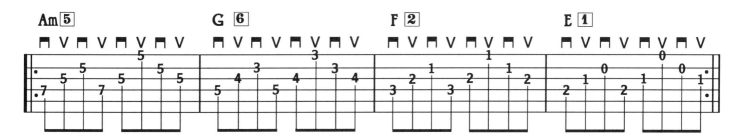

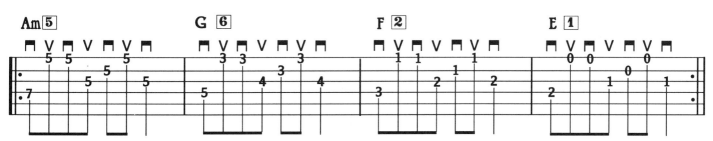

CHORD POSITIONS (Numbers in square boxes correspond to positions used in chord exercise.)

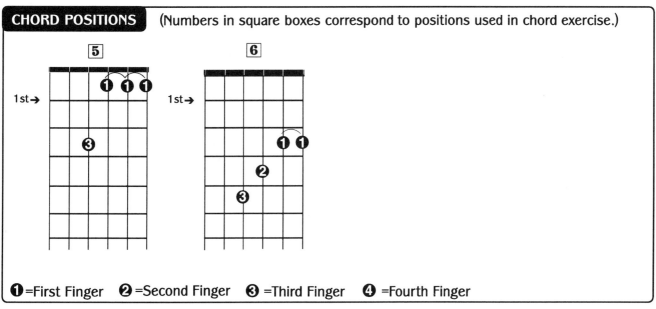

❶=First Finger ❷=Second Finger ❸=Third Finger ❹=Fourth Finger

Malagueña
(A Spanish Study)

3/4
Target Tempo:
♩ = 180
Key of E

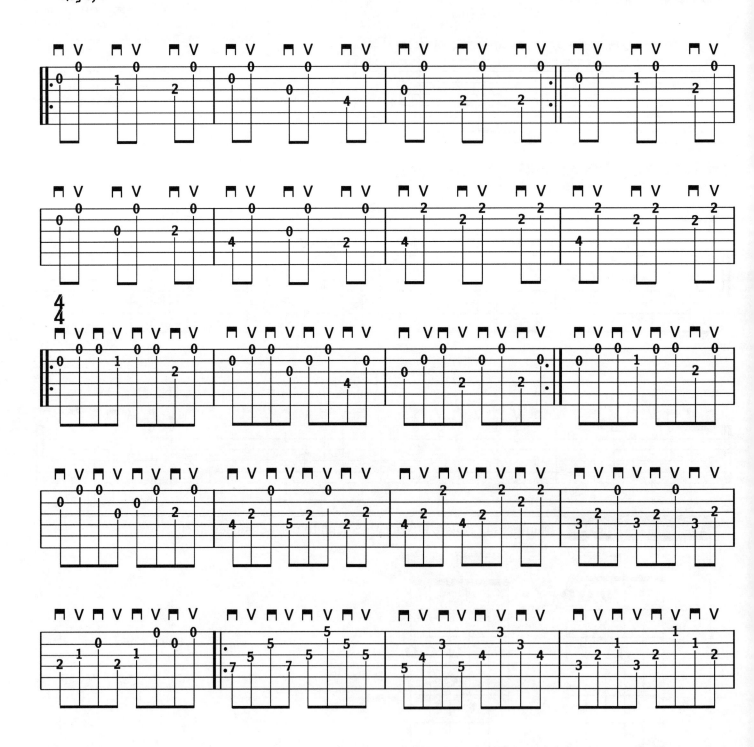

Malagueña
(A Spanish Study) (Continued)

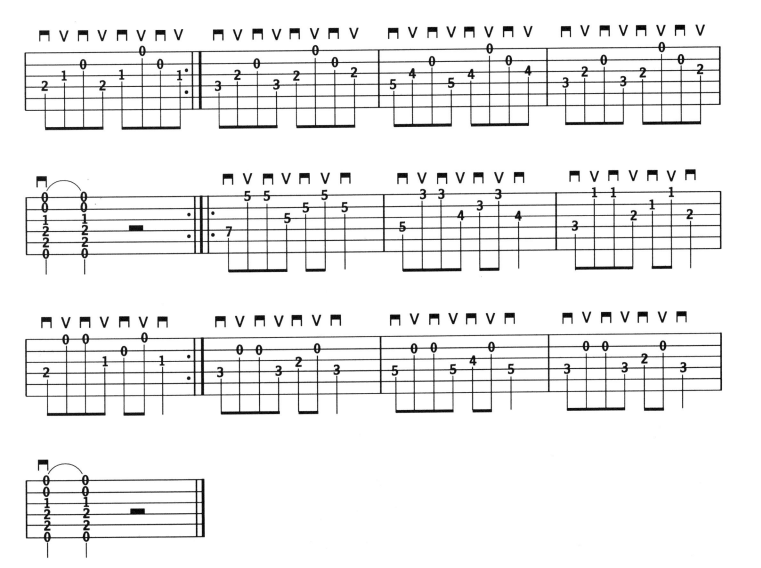

Crosspicking Jazz/Ragtime Style

Dill Pickle Rag

Beaumont Rag

Cotton Patch Rag

Dill Pickle Rag
Preparatory Study Notes

General Guidelines: Experiment by interchanging the chord exercises with the original piece. Make sure that you're fitting them into the same chordal phrases. You might also want to try plugging in other patterns over these same chord positions. Play this tune with the classic ragtime feel by accenting the first and third notes of each measure.

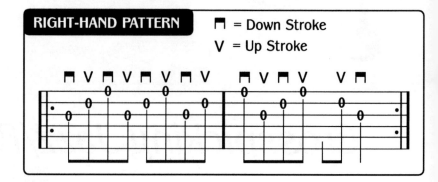

RIGHT-HAND PATTERN WITH CHORD EXERCISE

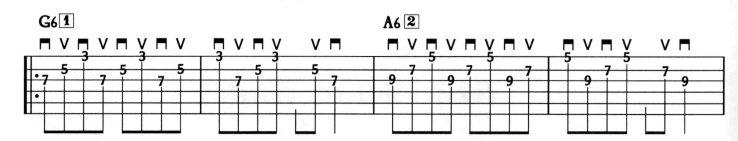

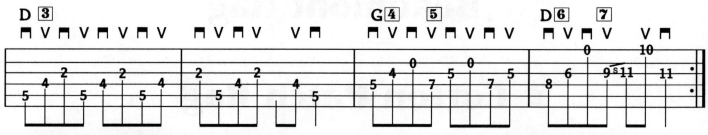

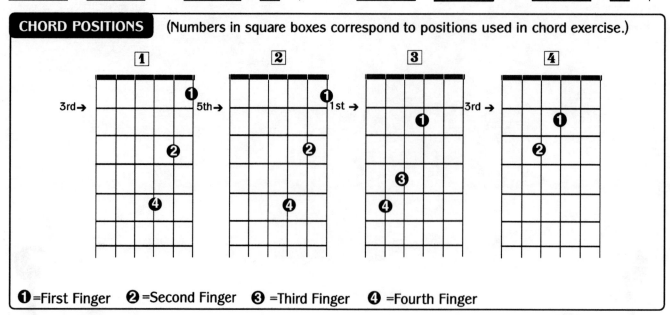

CHORD POSITIONS (Numbers in square boxes correspond to positions used in chord exercise.)

❶=First Finger ❷=Second Finger ❸=Third Finger ❹=Fourth Finger

Dill Pickle Rag
Preparatory Study Notes (cont.)

RIGHT-HAND PATTERN   ⊓ = Down Stroke
                           V = Up Stroke

Of Noted Interest: As is true of most other ragtime tunes, "Dill Pickle Rag" was originally written on piano. Play it at a moderate ragtime pace with a syncopated feel.

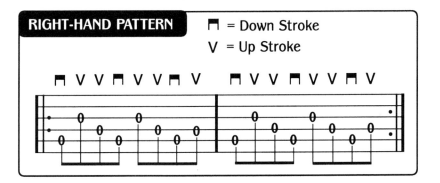

RIGHT-HAND PATTERN WITH CHORD EXERCISE

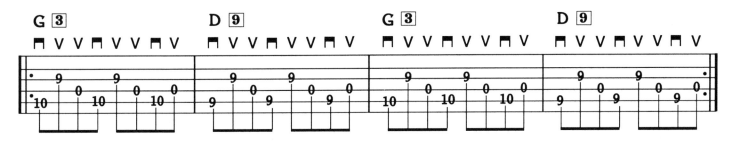

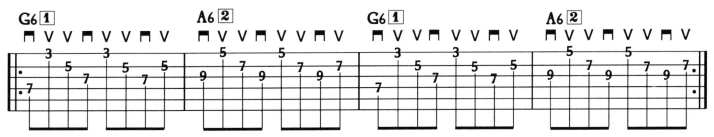

CHORD POSITIONS   (Numbers in square boxes correspond to positions used in chord exercise.)

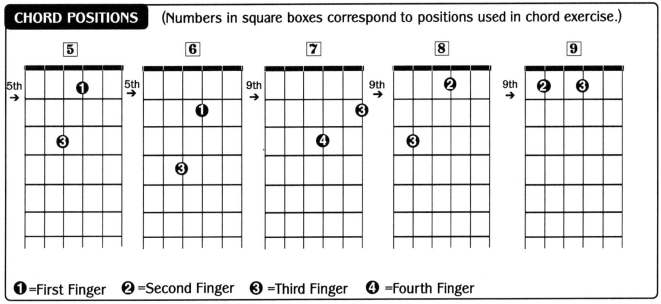

❶=First Finger   ❷=Second Finger   ❸=Third Finger   ❹=Fourth Finger

Jazz/Ragtime Style

Dill Pickle Rag

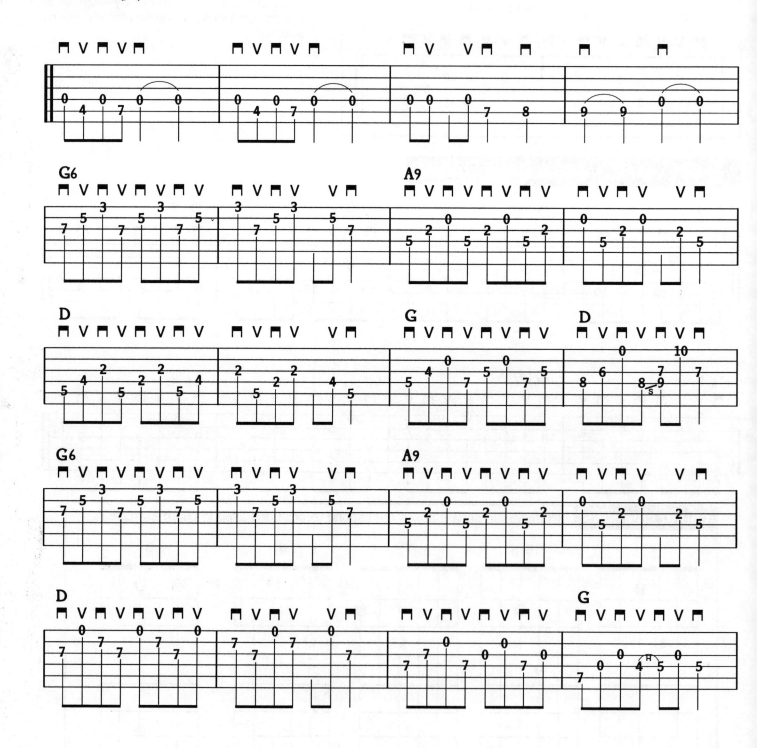

Dill Pickle Rag (Continued)

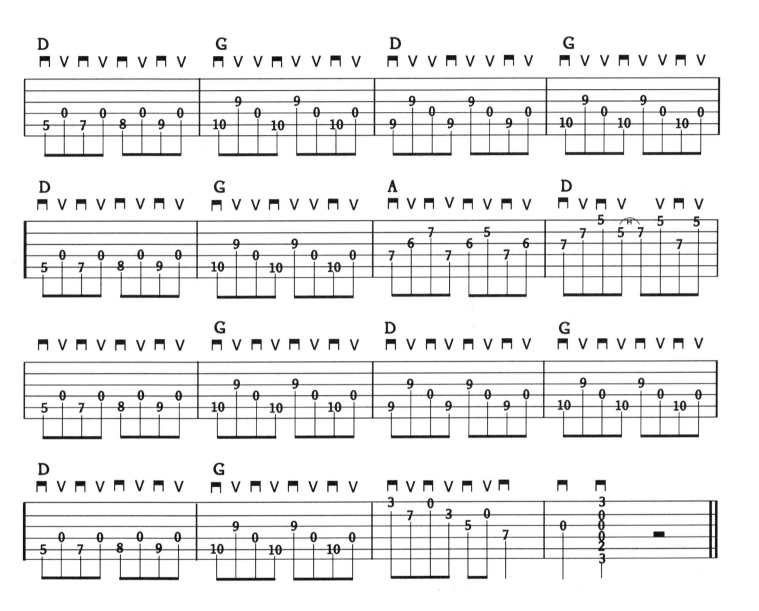

Beaumont Rag
Preparatory Study Notes

General Guidelines: The A part is played in a melodic banjo fashion. This approach involves playing the melody without attacking the same string twice. Try taking melodies you're familiar with and creating your own melodic banjo arrangements on guitar.

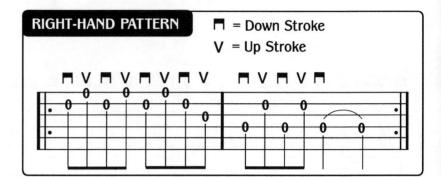

DIFFICULT PASSAGES

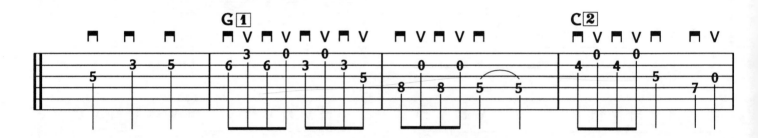

CHORD POSITIONS   (Numbers in square boxes correspond to positions used in chord exercise.)

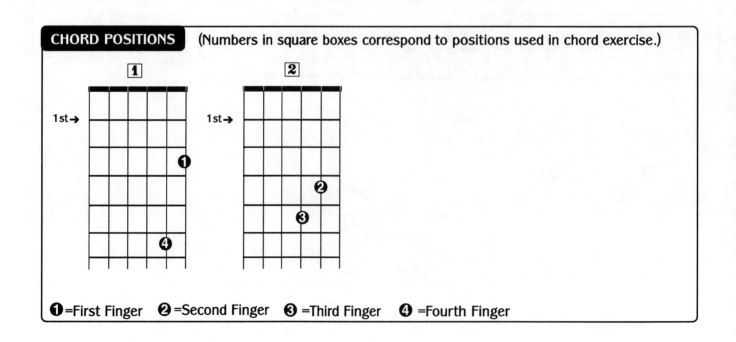

❶=First Finger   ❷=Second Finger   ❸=Third Finger   ❹=Fourth Finger

Beaumont Rag
Preparatory Study Notes

RIGHT-HAND PATTERN ⊓ = Down Stroke
V = Up Stroke

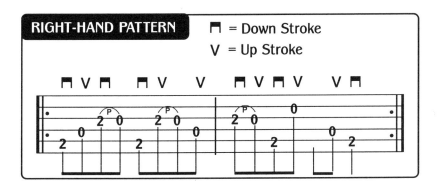

Of Noted Interest: A Texas-Style fiddle tune with a ragtime syncopation, made popular by artists such as Doc Watson and Dan Crary. Ray Valla has an excellent arrangement of this piece in his *Deluxe Bluegrass Mandolin Method.*

RIGHT-HAND PATTERN WITH CHORD EXERCISE

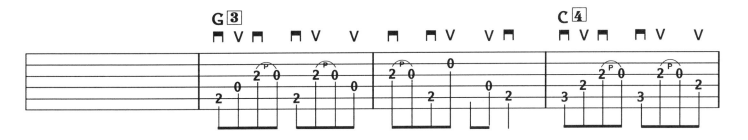

CHORD POSITIONS (Numbers in square boxes correspond to positions used in chord exercise.)

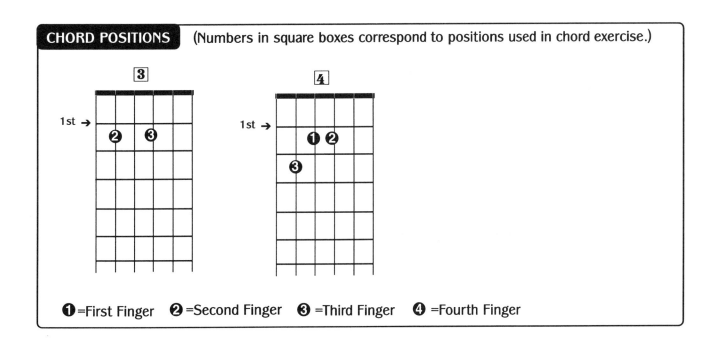

❶=First Finger ❷=Second Finger ❸=Third Finger ❹=Fourth Finger

Beaumont Rag

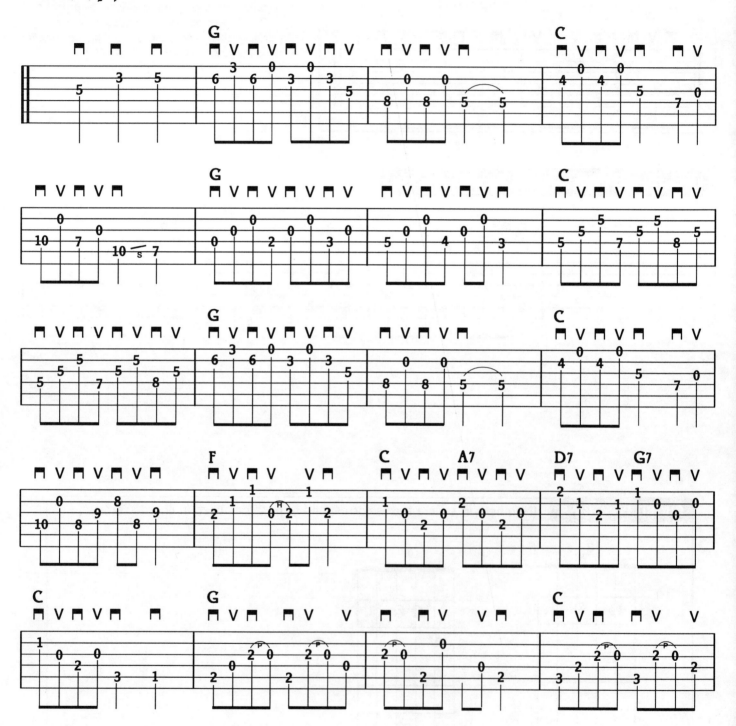

Beaumont Rag (Continued)

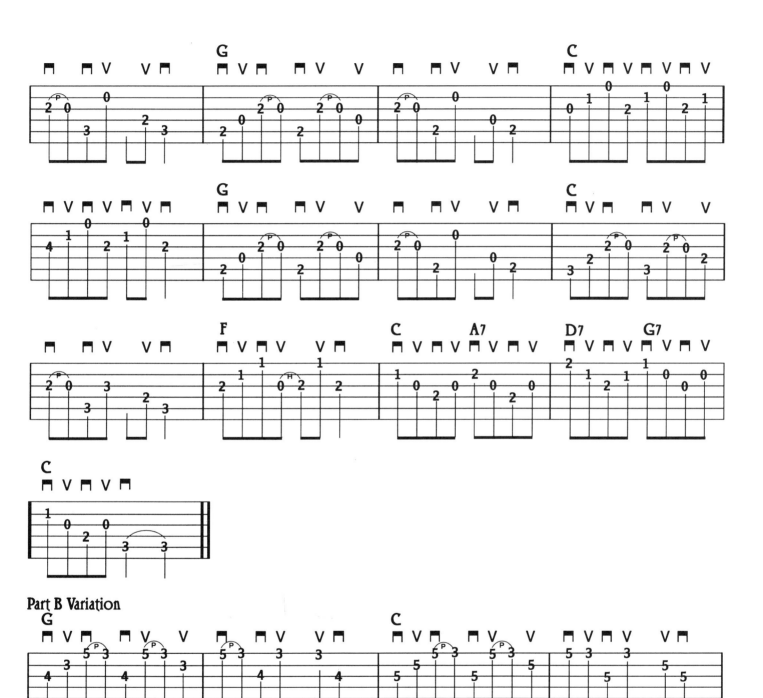

Part B Variation

Beaumont Rag (Continued)

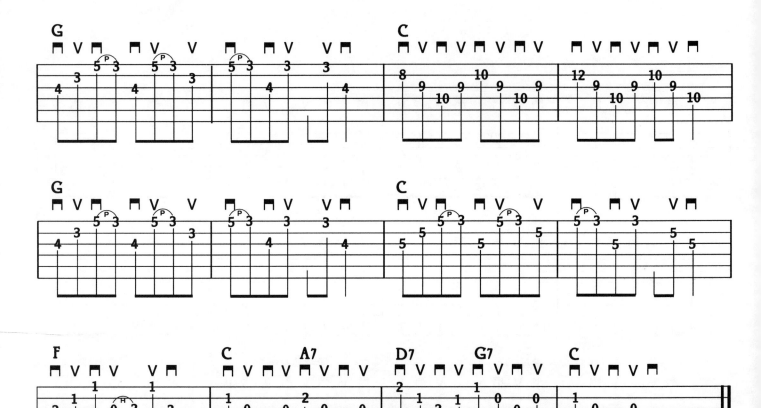

Cotton Patch Rag
Preparatory Study Notes

General Guidelines: This tune is also arranged in a melodic banjo fashion (as was Beaumont Rag). After accomplishing this piece, you'll be well on your way to becoming a crosspicking master guitarist. Be sure you're completely comfortable with the exercises before attempting to play the tune. There should be no pauses between the changes.

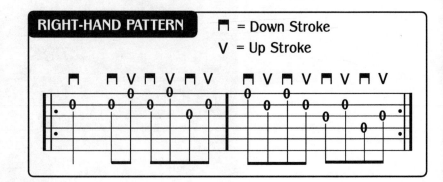

RIGHT-HAND PATTERN WITH CHORD EXERCISE

Difficult Passages

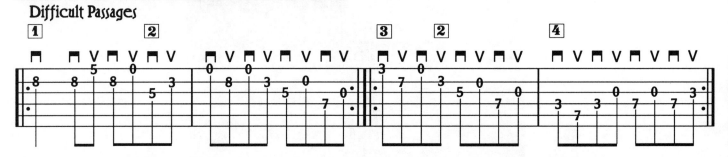

C Scale In Melodic Form

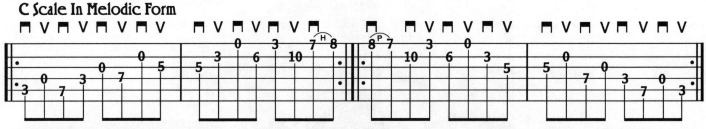

CHORD POSITIONS   (Numbers in square boxes correspond to positions used in chord exercise.)

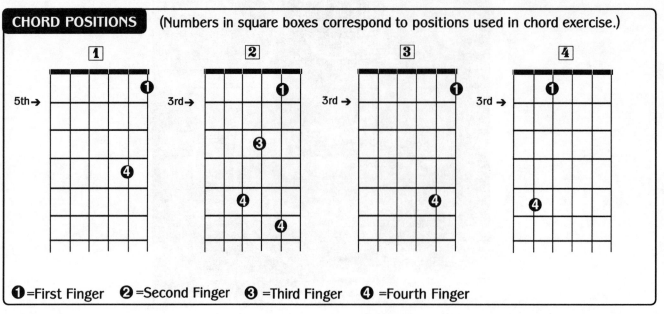

❶=First Finger   ❷=Second Finger   ❸=Third Finger   ❹=Fourth Finger

Cotton Patch Rag
Preparatory Study Notes

RIGHT-HAND PATTERN ⊓ = Down Stroke
V = Up Stroke

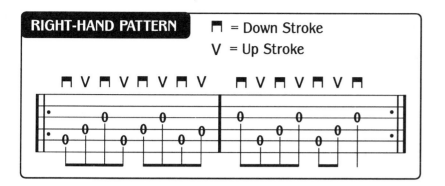

Of Noted Interest: A popular Texas-Style Fiddle tune. Tiny Moore, mandolinist for Bob Willis & His Texas Playboys, played this one at its highest level. Listen to Texas-Style fiddle players to gain endless ideas for flatpicking guitar.

RIGHT-HAND PATTERN WITH CHORD EXERCISE

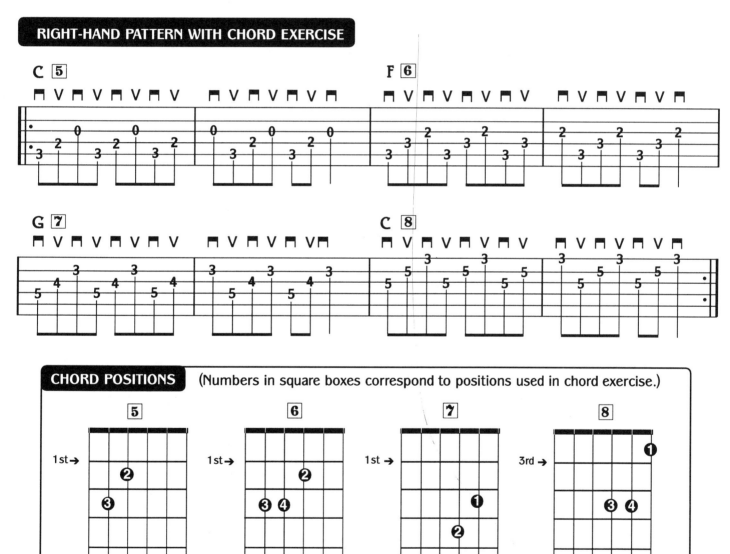

CHORD POSITIONS (Numbers in square boxes correspond to positions used in chord exercise.)

❶ =First Finger ❷ =Second Finger ❸ =Third Finger ❹ =Fourth Finger

Cotton Patch Rag

4/4
Target Tempo:
♩ = 175
Key of C

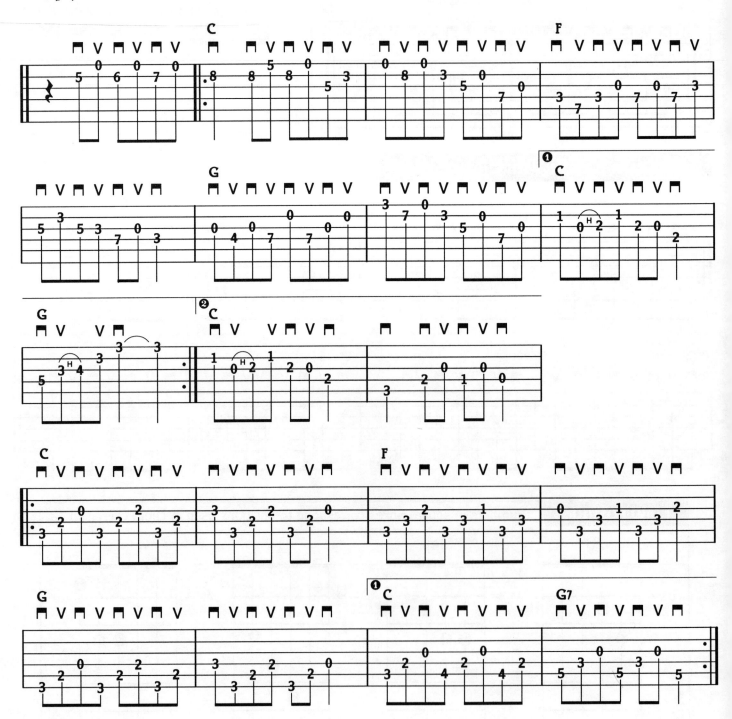

Cotton Patch Rag (Continued)

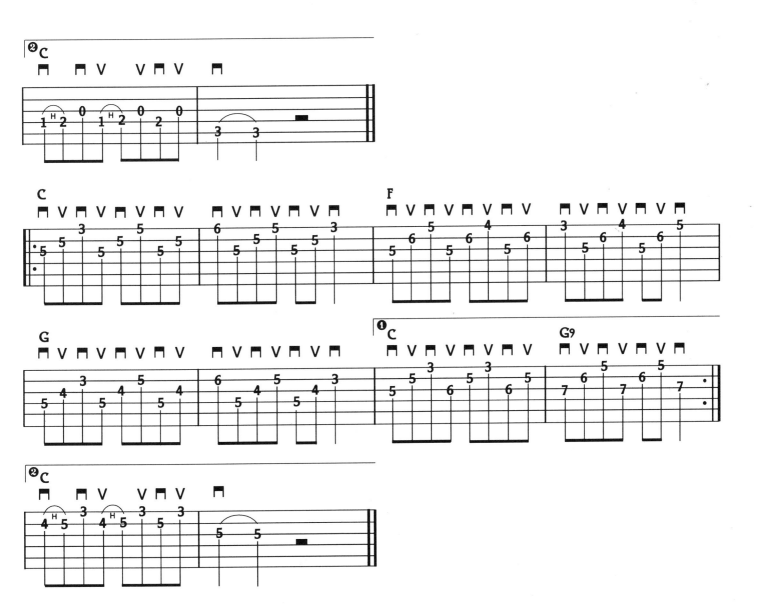

Vintage
Martin
Slotted

Crosspicking Songbook Section

Little Rock Getaway
Alabama Jubilee
Arkansas Traveler
Cripple Creek
Devil's Dream
Flop Eared Mule
Loch Laven Castle
Old Joe Clark
Ragtime Annie
Red Haired Boy
Sailor's Hornpipe
St. Anne's Reel
Turkey in the Straw

Little Rock Getaway
(Variation 1)

Music by Joe Sullivan

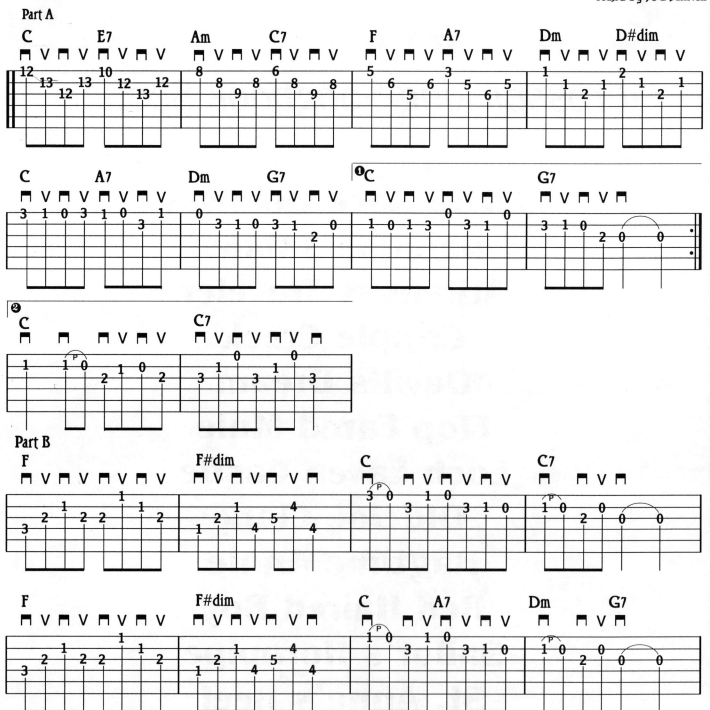

Little Rock Getaway
(Variation 1 Cont.)

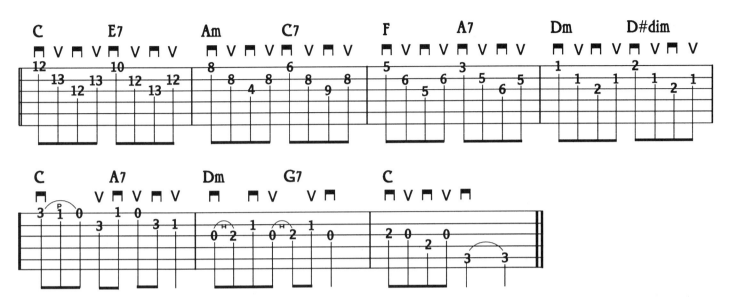

Little Rock Getaway
(Variation 2)

Part A

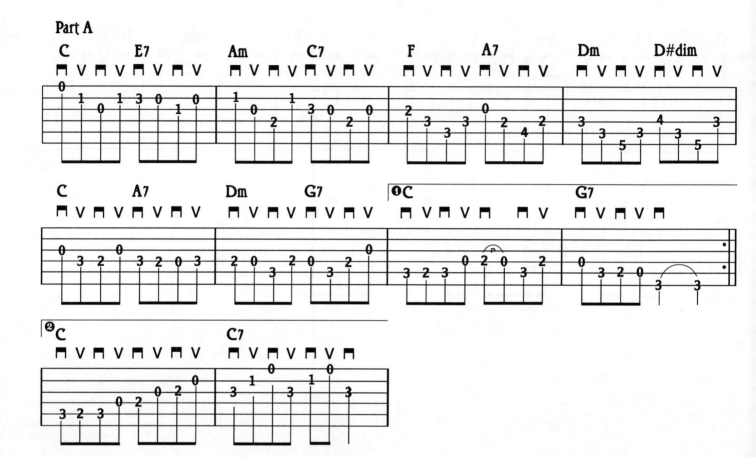

Alternate Last Two Measures of Part A (Variation 2)

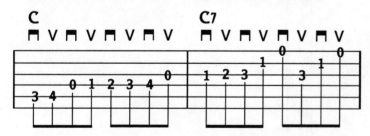

Little Rock Getaway
(Variation 2 Cont.)

Part B

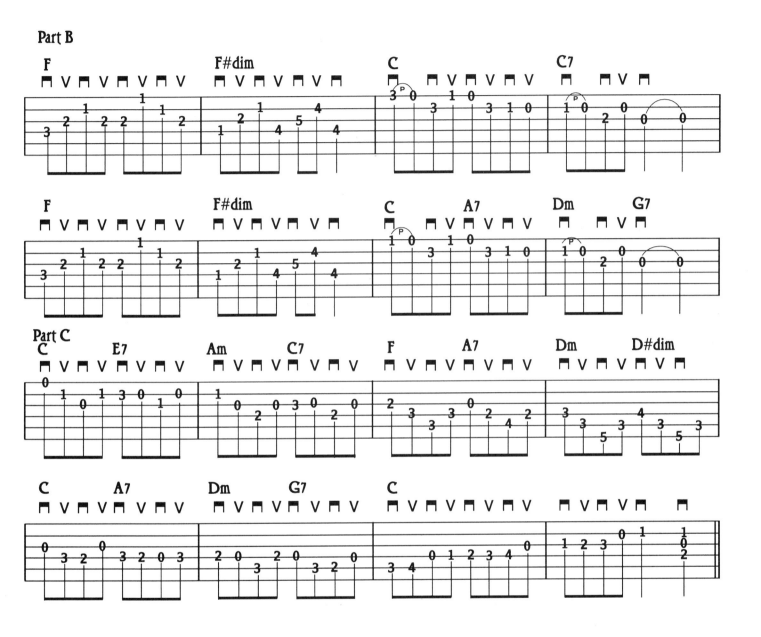

Alabama Jubilee

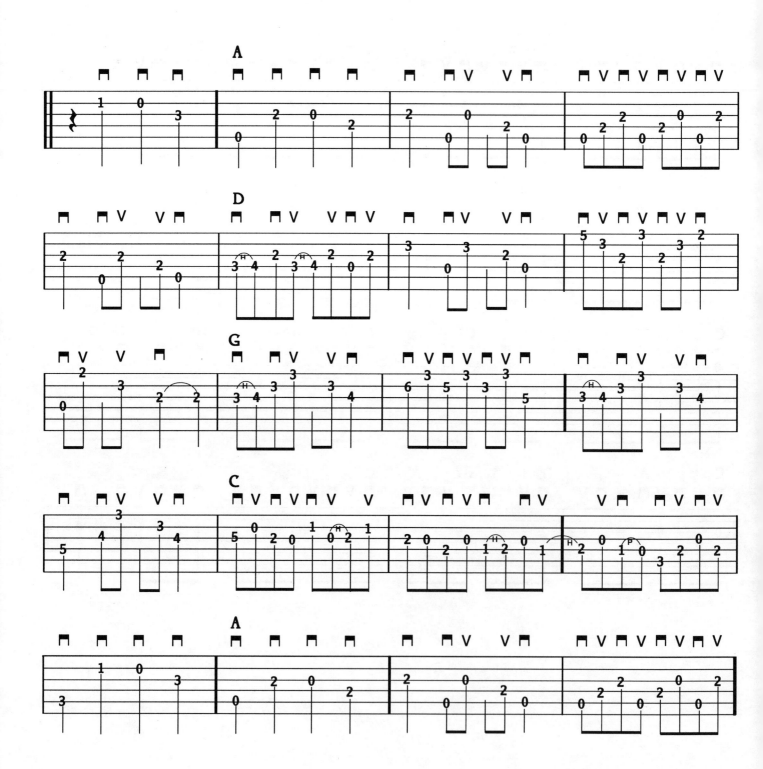

Alabama Jubilee
(Continued)

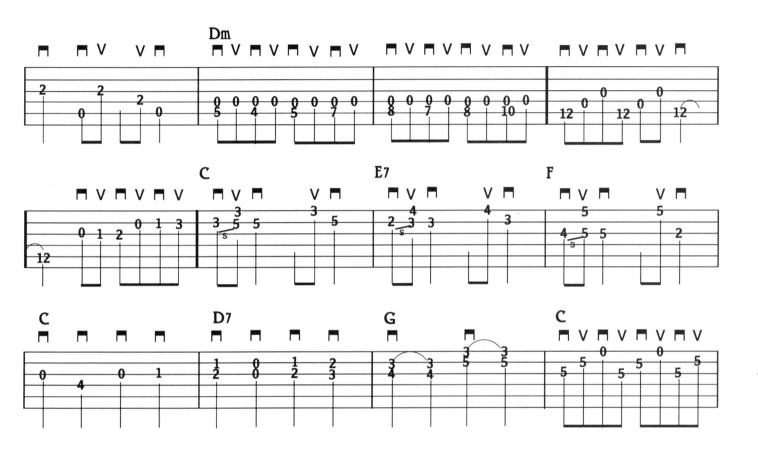

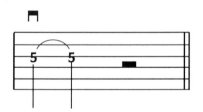

Arkansas Traveler

Arkansas Traveler (B Part Variation)

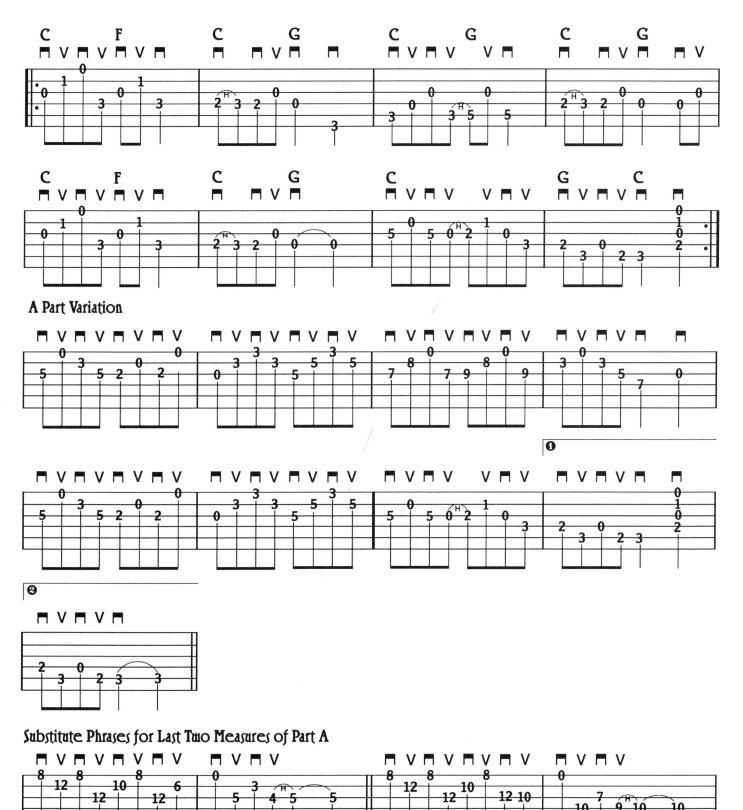

A Part Variation

Substitute Phrases for Last Two Measures of Part A

Cripple Creek

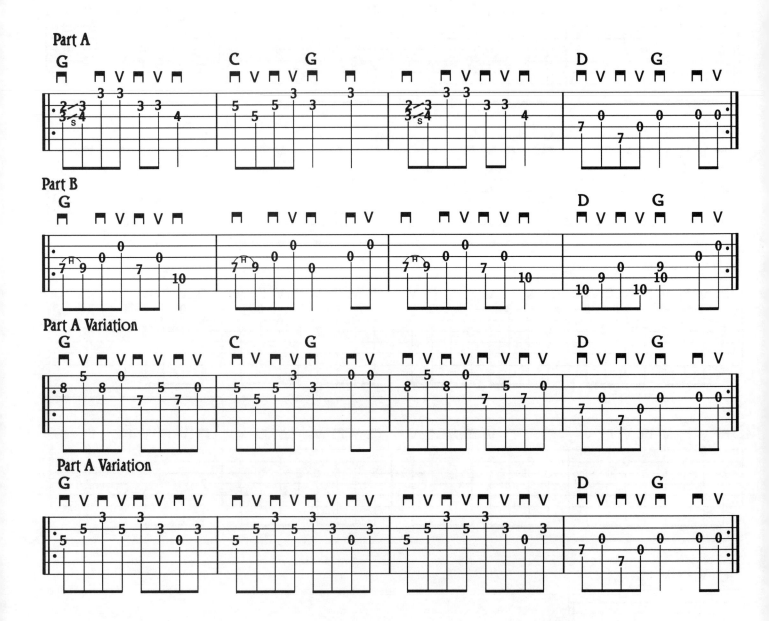

Devil's Dream

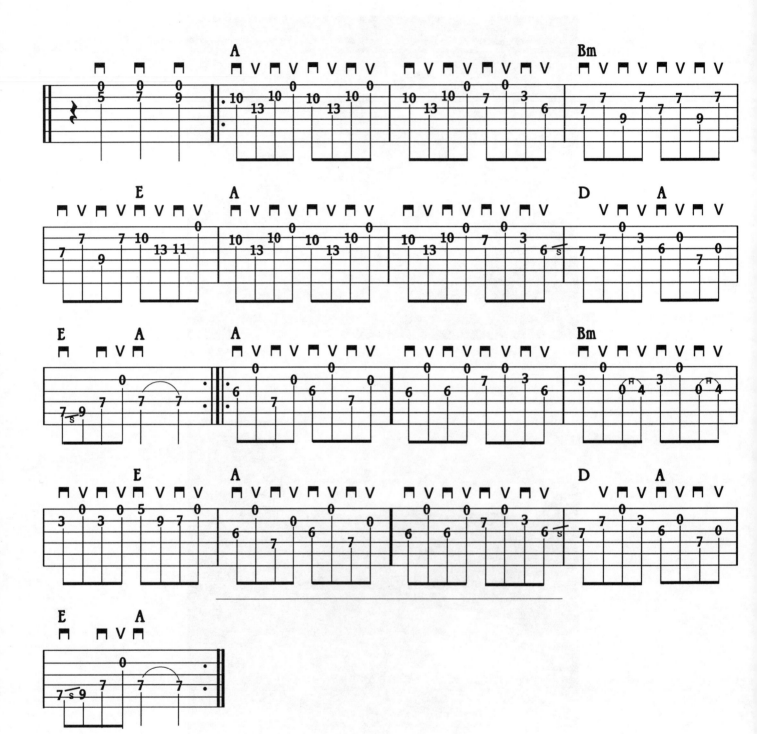

Flop Eared Mule

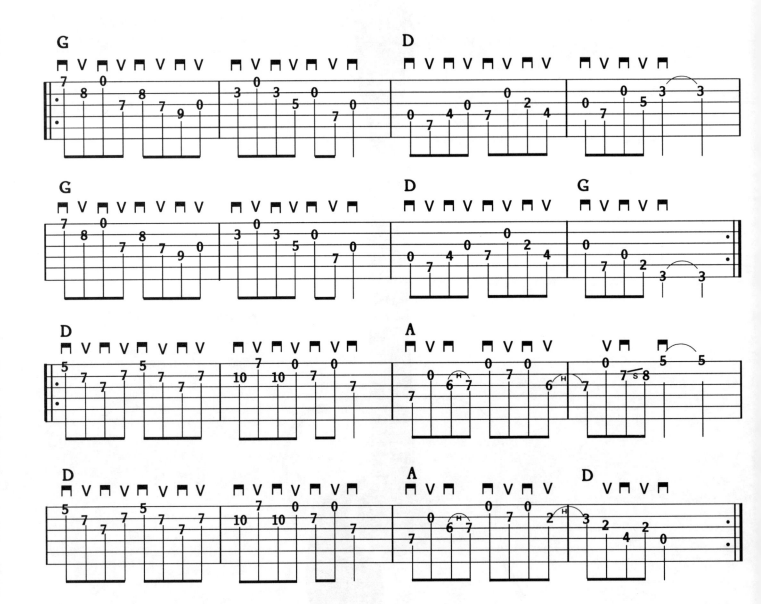

1939 Gibson
Advanced
Jumbo

Lach Lauven Castle

Lach Lauven Castle
(Continued)

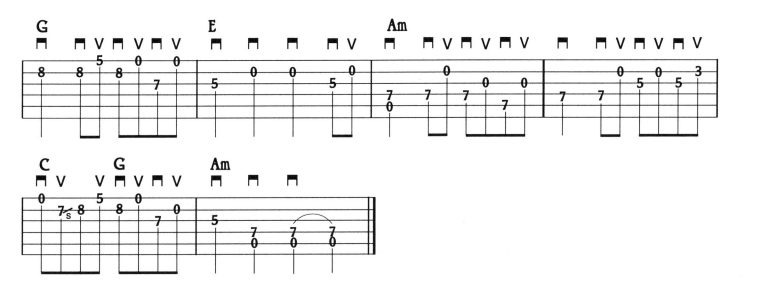

Old Joe Clark

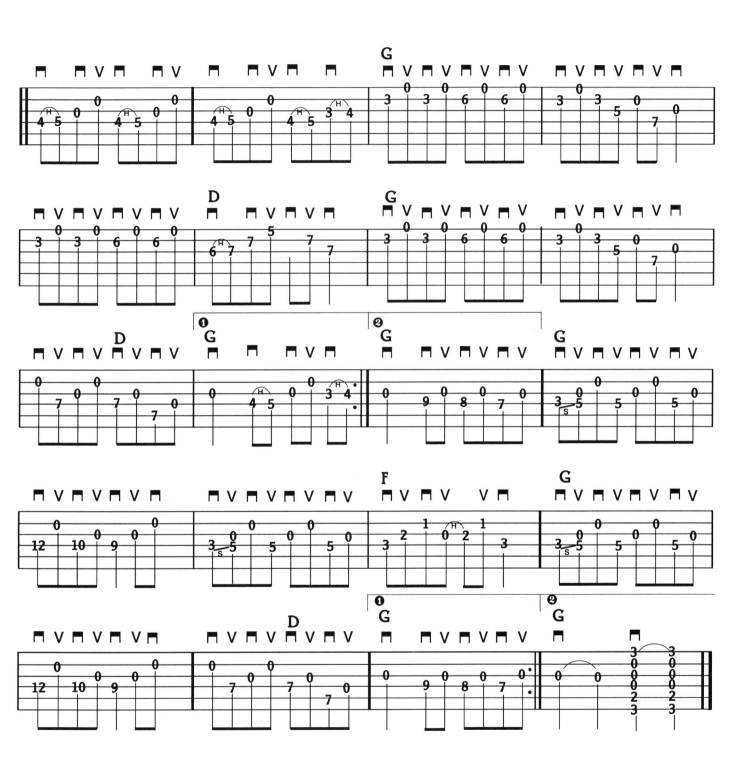

Ragtime Annie

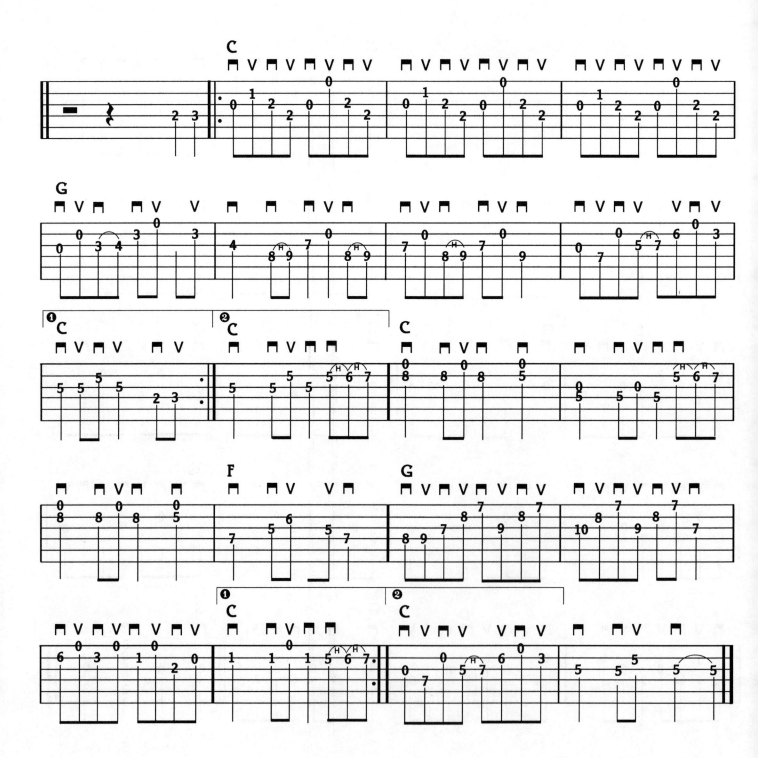

Red Haired Boy

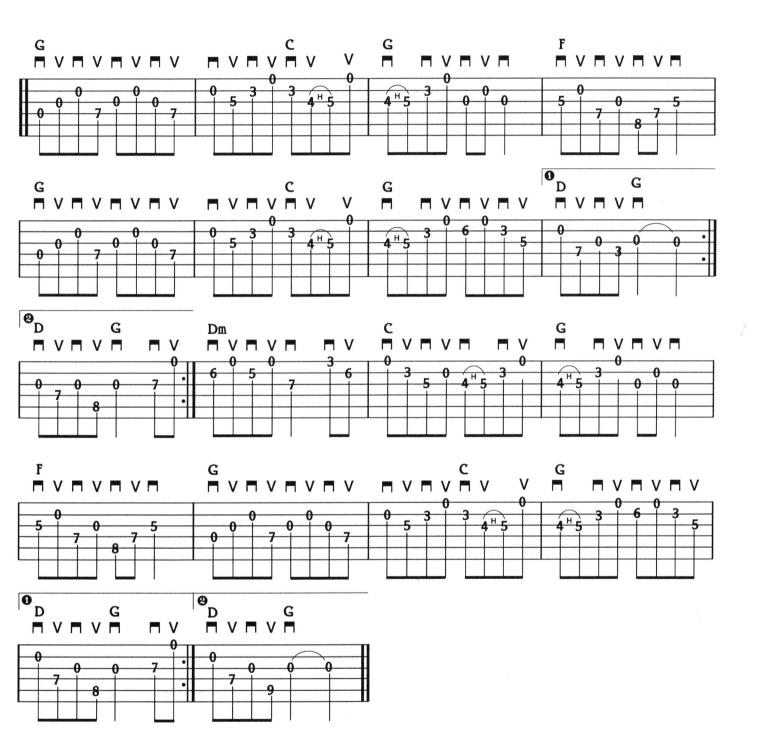

Sailor's Hornpipe

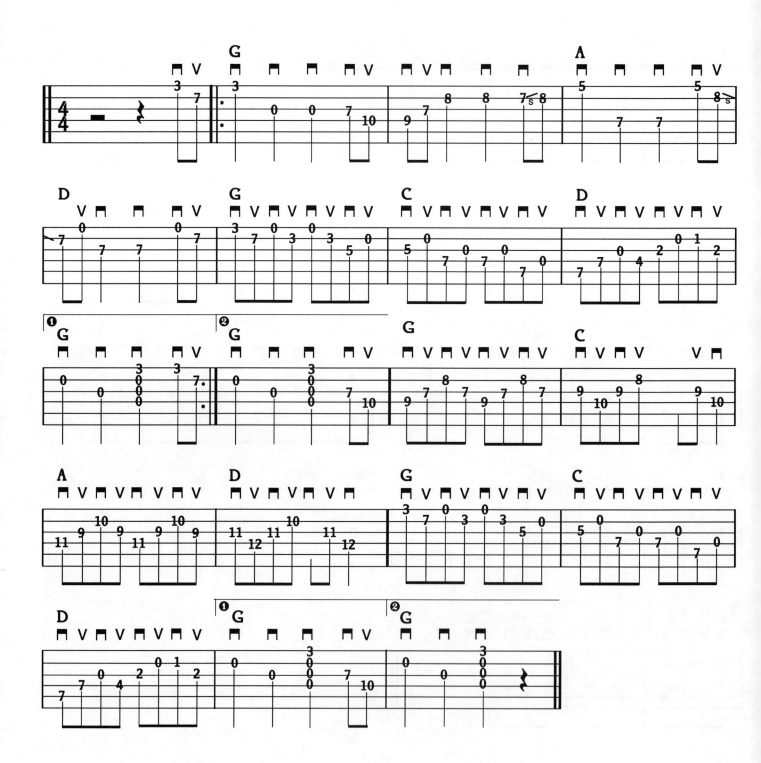

OFFICIAL SCENIC HISTORIC MARKER

LINCOLN

Spanish-speaking settlers established a town here in the 1850's, after the U. S. Army began to control the Mescalero Apaches. First known as Las Placitas del Rio Bonito, the name of the community was changed to Lincoln when Lincoln County was created in 1869.

TORREON

One of Lincoln's earliest structures. Built in the 1850's, its thick walls protected Spanish-Americans against the Apaches. In Lincoln Co. War Murphy's sharpshooters were here stationed. In 1937 Chaves County Historical Society undertook restoration of tower.

OLD LINCOLN COUNTY MEMORIAL COMMISSION 1950

St. Anne's Reel

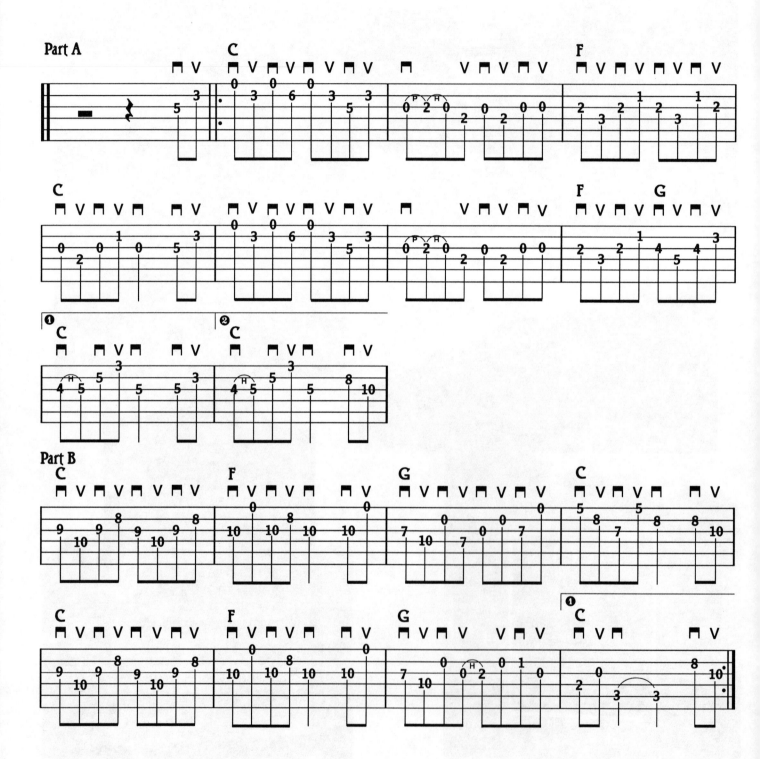

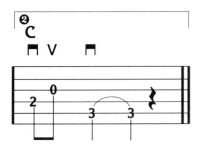

Mossman
Golden Era

Turkey In The Straw
(Variation 1)

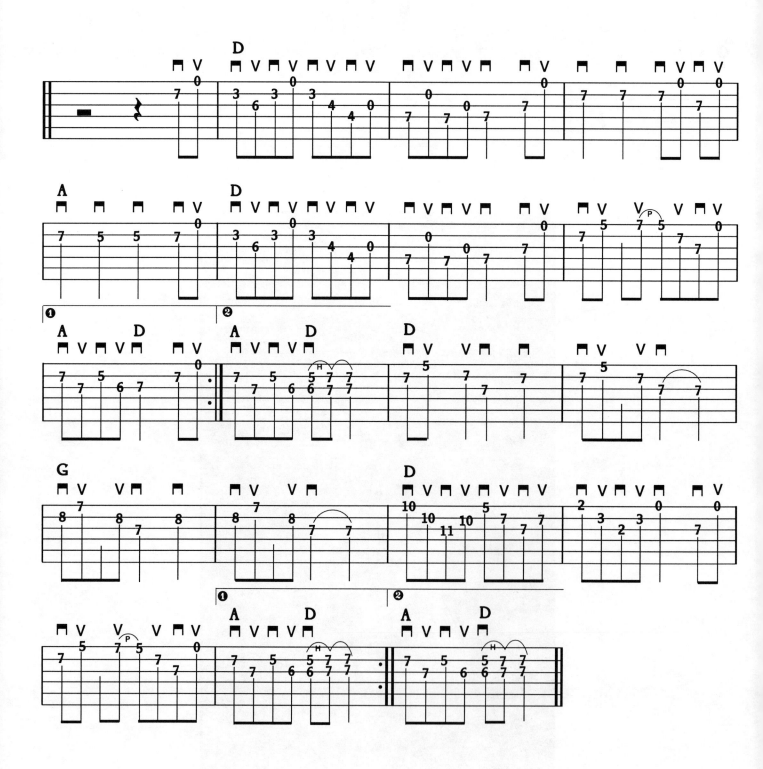

Turkey In The Straw
(Variation 2)

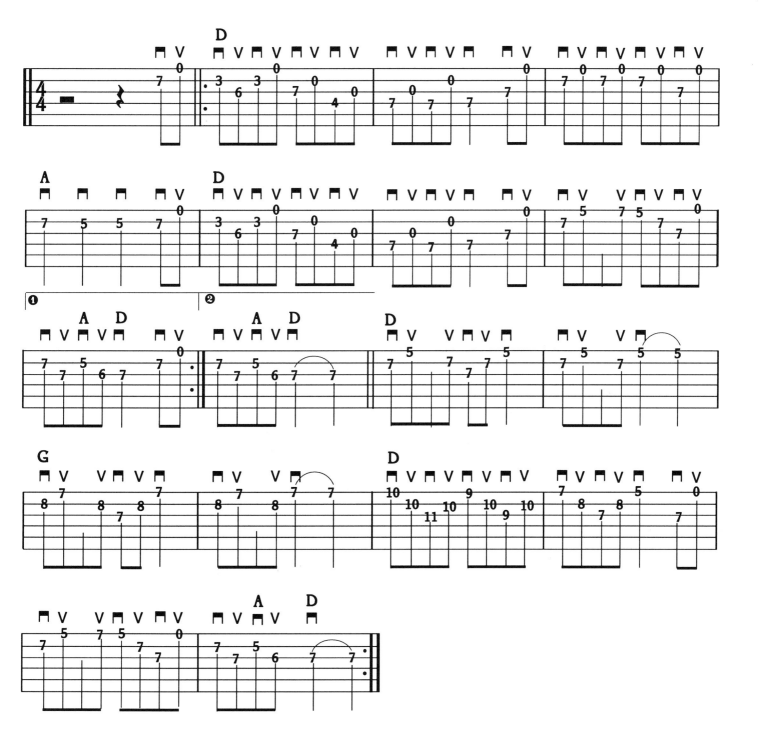

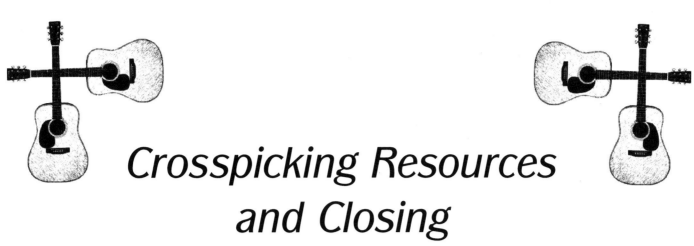

Crosspicking Resources and Closing

Conclusion

Suggested Listening

Further Study

Resources

Conclusion

The many crosspicking tunes and exercises you've accomplished, after completing this book, should give you a jumping-off point for developing many other possibilities; these innovations can only be accomplished through your unique musical perspective. Experiment! Try applying the many rolls and patterns to other melodies. When playing behind vocalists or instrumentalists, try some crosspicking patterns as backup variations. Listen to other guitarists with an assiduous ear. Many guitar masters have employed crosspicking, although some only minutely, in their playing: Dan Crary, Clarence White, Steve Kaufman, Norman Blake, Tony Rice are only a few of the many. The most outstanding mandolin crosspicking exponent, who has left a legacy of crosspicking tunes from the 1950s to today, is Jesse McReynolds. Buy every recording of Jesse's that you can get your hands on. Jesse has taken crosspicking into new dimensions for decades. He infuses crosspicking with an air of elegance yet to be matched. A great way to expand your guitar horizons is to open your ears to other instrumentalists besides guitarists. In our "Suggested Listening" section, watch for many references to both guitarists and mandolinists who have contributed to the expansion of crosspicking technique.

Everyone has their own musical journey. No two musicians have ever followed the exact same path. We are all a culmination of the listening influences and music books we've studied. Just like a painting, a song is interpreted differently by every musician that performs it. Even if the notes are played exactly in the same place, so many other shades of difference come into play. For instance: the volume, the attack, the medium utilized (type of strings, picks or instrument), the feel, and many other nuances will affect the outcome of the interpreted piece. So, discover your own journey and remember, be as it may, there is no such thing as being a mirror image of another musician. Don't stop learning! The journey only begins where you've left off.

Mickey Cochran
Multi-String Acoustic Instrumentalist
Mickey is a devotee of acoustic music...he believes in and promotes every aspect of acoustic music in most all venues. He is now owner and president of Folk of the Wood (www.folkofthewood.com) which specializes in new and used acoustic instruments along with instructional material published by Mel Bay.

Mickey states: "I have played acoustic music, without amplification, professionally for over 20 years. And, since I've always enjoyed sharing my knowledge with others, I decided to become more involved in supporting everyone's efforts in improving their acoustic musicianship by writing for Mel Bay Publications. Learning is a lifelong process that we all, as acoustic artists, should consider in our daily efforts to improve...we should never feel, within one lifetime, that we've reached the pinnacle."

While working as a full-time acoustic musician (6 nights a week for 12 years in one restaurant at Indian Cliffs Ranch/Cattleman's Steakhouse), he attended journalism school with a focus on photography and computer graphics. Mickey graduated from UTEP with a Journalism degree in 1989. Mickey is now devoted to promoting acoustic music and assisting others in their learning endeavors.

A Selection of Suggested Listening

A sampling of my personal favorites. Many of these recordings may no longer be available. Although, they may soon be reissued on CD. I've included both mandolin and guitar dominated

ARTIST	RECORDING	RECORD LABEL
Norman Blake	*Whiskey Before Breakfast*	Rounder Records
	Back Home in Sulphur Springs	Rounder Records
	Slow Train Through Georgia	Rounder Records
	Full Moon on the Farm	Rounder Records
	Lighthouse on the Shore	Rounder Records
	Nashville Blues	Rounder Records
	Original Underground Music from the Mysterious South	Rounder Records
	Just Gimme Somethin' I'm Used To	Shanachie Records
with Nancy Blake	*Blind Dog*	Rounder Records
	Natasha's Waltz	Rounder Records
	The Norman and Nancy Blake Compact Disc	Rounder Records
with Red Rector	*Norman Blake & Red Rector*	County
with Jethro Burns	*Jethro Burns, Norman Blake Sam Bush, Tut Taylor*	Flying Fish
Sam Bush	*Late As Usual*	Rounder Records
	Glamour and Grits	Sugar Hill Records
with New Grass Revival	*New Grass Revival*	Starday
	When the Storm is Over	Flying Fish Records
	Fly Through the Country	Flying Fish Records
	Too Late to Turn Back Now	Flying Fish Records
	The Festival Tapes	Flying Fish Records
	Barren County	Flying Fish Records
	Commonwealth	Flying Fish Records
	On the Boulevard	Sugar Hill Records
	New Grass Revival	EMI America
	Hold to a Dream	EMI America
	Friday Night in America	EMI America
with Alan Munde	*Poor Richard's Almanac*	American Heritage
	Sam and Alan Together Again For The First Time	Ridge Runner

A Selection of Suggested Listening

ARTIST	RECORDING	RECORD LABEL
Sam Bush (cont.) with Jerry Douglas	*Under the Wire* *Everything Is Gonna Work Out Fine*	MCA Rounder
Jimmy Gaudreau	*The Gaudreau Mandolin Album*	Puritan Records

David Grisman
 	
with Old and In the Way
 	
with Tony Rice
	The David Grisman Quintet
	Early Dawg
	The David Grisman
	      Rounder Compact Disc
	The David Grisman Quintet
	      Quintet '80
	Hot Dawg
	Mando Mondo
	
	Old and In the Way
	That High Lone Sound - Vol. 1
	
	Tone Poems
		Rhino Records
		Sugar Hill Records
		
		Rounder Records
		
		Warner Bros.
		Horizon Music
		      Warner Bros.
		
		Rounder Records
		Acoustic Disc
		
		Acoustic Disc

Doyle Lawson	*Tennessee Dream*	County
Dave Martini	*Mr. Mandolin Man* *Mr. Mandolin Man Picks Again* *Sounds of the Mandolin Man*	Stoneway STY 126 Stoneway STY 134 Stoneway STY 174
Jesse McReynolds with Jim & Jesse with Allen Shelton	*Airmail Special* *Mandolin Workshop* *The Jim & Jesse Story* *Epic Bluegrass Hits* *In The Tradition* *Music Among Friends* *Shelton Special*	Rebel Records Hilltop CMH Rounder Records Rounder Records Rounder Records Rounder Records

 # A Selection of Suggested Listening

ARTIST	RECORDING	RECORD LABEL
Steve Smith	*Distant Lands* *Other Places, Times & Lives* *Desert Night*	Desert Night Music Desert Night Music Desert Night Music
Country Cooking	*Country Cooking* *26 Bluegrass Originals*	Rounder Records Rounder Records
Roland White	*Appalachian Swing!* *Kentucky Colonels: 1965-67* *Kentucky Colonels: Long Journey...*	Rounder Records Rounder Records
Nitty Gritty Dirt Band	*Will the Circle be Unbroken*	Liberty Records
Various Artists:	*Flatpicking Guitar Festival*	Kicking Mule
Russ Barenberg	*Moving Pictures*	Rounder Records
Dan Crary	*Jammed If I Do* *Bluegrass Guitar* *Lady's Fancy*	Sugar Hill Records Sugar Hill Records Rounder Records
Tony Rice	*Acoustics* *Manzanita*	Rounder Records Rounder Records
Steve Kaufman	*Not Much Work for Saturday*	Independent
Leo Kottke	*6 and 12 String Guitar*	Rhino

A Selection for Further Study

Collecting and studying an extensive library of guitar instruction material will assist you in future efforts of becoming an accomplished guitarist. If you do not know how to read music, allow yourself the opportunity by acquiring the suggested study material included here. It will transform you into a well-rounded guitarist and enable you to take on anything thrown your way. Consider also the importance of building a vast repertoire—by learning and memorizing many different songs, you'll be increasing your proficiency, knowledge of how songs are composed, ability to read tablature and standard notation, knowledge of chords and scales, along with possessing a selection of tunes that will fill any request.

Some of the books listed may be out of print. They are all included since many books fall in and out of print periodically. These books fall into many categories; the main division would be that some are methodology books, while others are songbooks. A methodology book instructs on how to approach the instrument in an effort to build technique; a songbook is more of a repository—a collection of songs that will build your repertoire.

FLATPICKING GUITAR FOR FURTHER STUDY

I. The Norman Blake Anthology

by Norman Blake; transcribed by Steve Kaufman

Flatpicking Guitar Magazine declares Norman Blake a legend, and includes him in the "first name club" on the Internet flatpicking news list. In posting to the list, the magazine maintains, one only needs mention the first name of such a legendary player to be instantly understood. Norman is a fine flatpicking guitarist and writer of songs that seem burnished in the old-time tradition the moment they are created.

Norman's musical resume includes stints on most of the old-time radio broadcasts (including the Grand Ole Opry), tours with Kris Kristofferson, Johnny Cash, and Joan Baez, and four consecutive Grammy nominations. In addition to his own sizeable body of recorded work, either solo or with his wife Nancy,

Norman has played on many notable recordings including Bob Dylan's Nashville Skyline, the Nitty Gritty Dirt Band's Will the Circle Be Unbroken, John Hartford's Steam Powered Aeroplane, and Steve Earle's Train A Comin'.

The Legacy of Doc Watson offers complete lyrics and melody lines to 40 original songs, written and notated just as Norman sings them. Often, the vocal version is followed by a second flatpicking solo edition in notation and tablature including introductions and solos within a given tune- all authorized by Norman himself! 200 wire-bound pages, illustrated with photos from a distinguished 30-year career. Intermediate in difficulty. 200 pages.

A Selection for Further Study

FLATPICKING GUITAR FOR FURTHER STUDY (Cont.)

II. Master Anthology of Flatpicking Guitar Solos Vol. 1

Mel Bay's solo anthology series, which includes both new pieces and some of the best previously published pieces from the latter half of the 20th century, is designed to enhance the repertoire of the intermediate to advanced instrumentalist. This collection presents a substantial collection of 50 challenging flatpicking guitar solos by many of the finest flatpicking guitarists of the latter half of the 20th century, including Mike Christiansen, David Grier, Mark Cosgrove, Norman Blake, Gary Brewer, Robin Bullock, Dan Crary, Steve Kaufman, Mark O'Connor, and many others. Standard notation and tablature are offered for each piece. A set of two companion stereo CD's is included, making this an ideal sourcebook for serious students and professionals alike. The CDs include all of the tunes in the book except Doc's Rag by Doc Watson and Horseshoe Bend by Tim Stafford. 216 pages.

III. Bluegrass Guitar

by Tommy Flint

Bluegrass Guitar is both a method book and a collection of progressively arranged traditional and Southern mountain songs. Although primarily designed to be played with a flat pick, several right-hand playing styles are also represented. Many tunes are shown as both lyric versions to be sung with guitar accompaniment, and as flatpicking pick/strum guitar solos. Selections include: This Train; John Henry; On Top of Old Smokey; The Midnight Run; Deer Lick Creek; Bill Cheatham; Give Me That Old Time Religion; Skip to My Lou; and several Tommy Flint originals.

The author also offers lead guitar solo concepts for traditional tunes like: The Galway Piper; Liberty; Billy in the Low Ground; Leather Britches; and
 others. A short fingerstyle segment on "How to Play Bluegrass Banjo Style on the Guitar" closes the book. Throughout, the author displays an intuitive awareness of various left and right-hand techniques and their imaginative application. With the enclosed companion CD containing all of the selections and exercises in the book, this outstanding Mel Bay Value Line book offers the beginning to intermediate bluegrass guitarist a significant value. Printed in standard notation and tablature. 40 pages.

A Selection for Further Study

FLATPICKING GUITAR FOR FURTHER STUDY (Cont.)

IV. Classics for Flatpicking Guitar

by William Bay

A collection of classical pieces arranged for flatpicking guitar, together with a few modern flatpicking originals in the classical style by William Bay. Includes works by J. S. Bach, Dowland, Handel, Krieger, Mouret, Playford, Praetorius, Quantz, Rameau, Sanz, and St. Jacome, as well as music by two anonymous Renaissance lutenists - 21 pieces in all. All selections appear in standard notation and tablature with fingering and suggested guitar chords when appropriate. The companion CD includes all of the selections in the book. 32 pages.

V. Mel Bay's Complete Flatpicking Guitar Book

by Steve Kaufman

Written by Steve Kaufman, three time National Flatpicking Guitar Champion, this text is an information filled, fascinating study into contemporary flatpicking guitar. It includes bluegrass backup, arranging, flatpicking solos for bluegrass vocals, arranging instrumentals "from start to finish", and an excellent section on "Flatpickers Who Influence the Flatpickers." This book also contains many rousing Steve Kaufman flatpicking solos. Written in notation and tablature.

VI. Easy Flatpicking Guitar Solos

by Dick Weissman

This book is designed to help the beginning to intermediate flatpicking guitarist in developing control of the pick. The author introduces a number of traditional and ethnic styles and discusses various flatpicking techniques including up and down picking, crosspicking, and playing with a combination of pick and fingers. The approximately 30 progressively arranged pieces in the book are useful in learning to read both standard notation and tablature. Where practical, suggested chords are offered for a second guitarist. A companion CD is included- all at a great price!

VII. Flatpicking Tunes for 12-String Guitar

by William Bay

This book presents many favorite fiddle tunes expertly arranged for 12-string guitar. Presents Irish, French Canadian, Scottish, American, and traditional set dances, ballads, jigs, hornpipes, reels, and fiddle tunes. Selections include: Far from Home; Swallowtail Jig; The Cuckoo; Sea Breeze; Drowsy Maggie; Neapolitan Threshers; Harvest Moon Strathspey; Green Fields of America; Ivy Leaf Reel; and more. Written in standard notation and tablature. 48 pages.

A Selection for Further Study

FLATPICKING GUITAR FOR FURTHER STUDY (Cont.)

VIII. Flatpickin' The Gospels

by Steve Kaufman

In this book three time National Flatpicking Guitar Champion Steve Kaufman presents rousing guitar solos on 24 gospel favorites. Each song is shown with a melody part in notation and tablature, lyrics, an accompaniment part in tablature and a stirring flatpicking solo in notation and tablature. Selections include: Are You Washed in the Blood?; A Beautiful Life; Faith Of Our Fathers; The Glory Land Way; Heaven's Jubilee; In The Garden; Just A Closer Walk With Thee; Life's Railway To Heaven; The Lily Of The Valley; Near The Cross; Nearer, My God, To Thee; The Old Gospel Ship; The Old Rugged Cross; Old Time Religion; Precious Memories; Softly and Tenderly; Sweet By and By; Sweet Hour of Prayer; There Is Power In The Blood; The Unclouded Day; What A Friend; When The Roll Is Called Up Yonder; When The Saints Go Marching In; Where The Soul Never Dies.

IX. Kaufman's Collection of American Fiddle Tunes for Flatpicking Guitar

by Steve Kaufman

A massive collection of 250 delightful American fiddle tunes brilliantly arranged for flatpicked guitar. All of these tunes are written in guitar-friendly keys in notation and tab. On the companion double-CD set, Steve plays 85 of the tunes as written in the book, adding an improvised chorus or two for each. Intermediate in difficulty, the book includes an explanation of the guitar tablature system and the execution and notation of essential techniques such as bends, slides, hammer-ons and pull-offs. The tunes are thoughtfully printed in alphabetical order and include both standards and lesser-known fiddle melodies. Teachers take note- this book is a great source of sightreading material as well as a departure point for improvisation. 406 pp.

X. Hot Solos for Flatpick Guitarists

by Mark Cosgrove

A compilation of nine flatpicking solos by National Flatpicking Guitar Champion Mark Cosgrove. Three of these solos were winners at the National Flatpicking Championships in Winfield, Kansas. These songs are challenging and enjoyable. More importantly, for the potential flatpicking championship contender- these tunes contain some of the required ingredients for a national competition: crosspicking, open string or "floating passages," and sections which require a certain amount of stamina when played at speed. Written in standard notation and tablature with guitar accompaniment chords provided. 86 pp.

XI. Power Flatpicking Guitar

by Steve Kaufman

A masterful flatpicking technique book offering bluegrass licks, scales, basic chords, and solos in various positions up the neck in the keys of G, C, D, A, E, B-flat, and F. This book of basic technical studies presents only a few flatpicking repertoire pieces illustrating each concept and key. Features: Fisher's Hornpipe; Lonesome Road Blues; and The Bluegrass Boogie. Novice players will find the recording a great asset in learning this material. All studies and pieces are written in notation and tablature. 68 pp.

A Selection for Further Study

Gibson J-45

Breedlove SD-20

Guild AT5-2S

Taylor 415

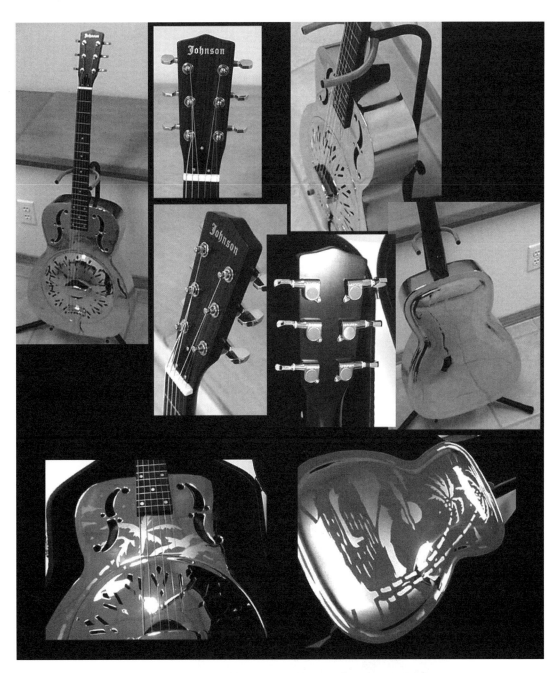

Johnson Hawaiian Sandblast

Guitar Crosspicking Technique
Guitar Crosspicking Technique

Visit us on the Web at www.melbay.com — E-mail us at email@melbay.com

Guitar Closing & Resources

Acoustic Music Resources

Acoustic Music Resource Websites

Elderly Instruments www.elderly.com
Mandolin Brothers www.mandolinbrothers.com
Gruhn Guitars www.gruhnguitars.com
Folk of the Wood www.folkofthewood.com
The Mandolin Cafe www.mandolincafe.com
Mugwumps www.mugwumps.com

Acoustic Magazines

Flatpicking Guitar Magazine www.flatpick.com
Bluegrass Unlimited www.bluegrassmusic.com
Banjo Newsletter www.banjonews.com

Instrument Manufacturers

Gibson Musical Instruments www.gibson.com
Breedlove Guitars www.breedloveguitars.com
Gallagher Guitars www.gallagherguitar.com
Tennessee Guitars www.crafterstn.com
Martin Guitars www.mguitar.com
Deering Banjos www.deeringbanjos.com
Goldtone Banjos www.goldtone.com
Weber Mandolins www.soundtoearth.com
Rigel Mandolins www.rigelmandolin.com
Phoenix Mandolins www.phoenixmandolins.com
Pimentel Guitars http://NS2.RT66.com/~Pimentel

Instructional Books & Videos

Mel Bay Publications www.melbay.com
•Check out our dealer listing•
Bayside Press www.Baysidepress.com

PHOTO CREDITS:
Steve Szilagyi
Dave Matchette
Mickey Cochran